W9-CFT-666

Also by Virgil Suárez

Latin Jazz

The Cutter

Welcome to the Oasis & Other Stories

Havana Thursdays

As Editor

Iguana Dreams: New Latino Fiction

Paper Dance: 55 Latino Poets

Little Havana Blues:
A Cuban-American Literature Anthology

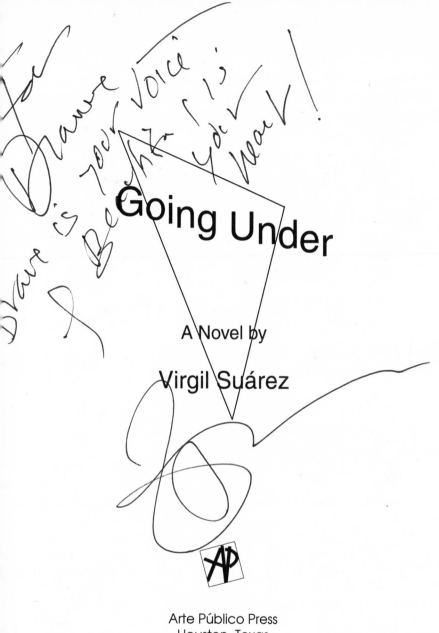

Going Under

A Novel by

Virgil Suárez

Arte Público Press
Houston, Texas
1996

Excerpts from this novel have appeared sometimes in different form in the following publications: *Bridges to Cuba/Puentes a Cuba*, edited by Ruth Behar, *Michigan Quarterly Review*, Volume 33, Number 4, Fall 1994, and *Currents from the Dancing River: Contemporary Latino Fiction, Nonfiction, and Poetry*, an anthology edited by Ray González, published by Harcourt Brace & Company, New York, 1994.

This volume is made possible through grants from the National Endowment for the Arts (a federal agency), the Andrew W. Mellon Foundation and the Lila Wallace-Reader's Digest Fund.

Recovering the past, creating the future

Arte Público Press
University of Houston
Houston, Texas 77204-2090

Cover art "Juan" by Ramón Delgadillo
Cover design by Gladys Ramirez

Suárez, Virgil, 1962–
    Going under / by Virgil Suárez.
       p.   cm.
    ISBN 1-55885-159-3 (cloth)
    1. Cuban Americans—Florida—Miami—Fiction. 2. Divorced men—Florida—Miami—Fiction. I. Title.
PS3569.U18G6   1996
813'.54—dc20   96-13699
                                CIP

The paper used in this publication meets the requirements of the American National Standard for Permanence of Paper for Printed Library Materials Z39.48-1984. ∞

This book is dedicated to

Wasabi *who was there when the spirit spoke,*

my wife Delia *who provided the love and understanding,*

my agent Elaine Markson *who encouraged,*

and publisher Nicolás Kanellos *who believes.*

Author's Note

This book would not have been possible without the help and encouragement from the following individuals: Phillip Quinn Morris, Christine Bell, Jim Shaffer, Mitchell Kaplan of Books & Books in Coral Gables, Florida, James Mosher, Federico Poey, Sr. and Jr., Bernardo Pestano, and George Primov of AGRIDEC, the Suárez-Alcázar-Poey family for the love and food.

Kufón kufó anundirá.
La avaricia rompe el saco.
Avarice corrupts.

—Abakuá Proverb

"We all live in countries
we cannot die in."

—after "Adultery"
a poem by James Dickey

Going Under

In Miami during the Last Days
of the Reagan Years

XAVIER CUEVAS found himself stuck in bumper-to-bumper expressway traffic. The lunchtime rush hour in Miami. Exasperated, he changed lanes, taking chances in his 240GL Volvo. An accident, he suspected and cut to the right-hand lane where the dense traffic moved at a faster pace. *Coagulate*, the word formed in his mind.

Undo this coagulation!

Xavier, the young, urban Cuban American. The YUCA, the equivalent of yuppie. Business at hand at all times. In haste, no time to waste. Twenty-four hours a day not being enough time. Seven days a week. No time to rest. For in this magic city of Miami, the Sun Capital, countless deals waited to be made, and whoever struck first, struck big by making the money.

Into the center lane. Behind an eighteen-wheel Mobil Oil rig. Nobody budged to let him in. Nobody gave him a chance. *Can't they see*, he thought, *can't they see I'm in a hurry?* Stuck indeed. Caught. Missing in action in Miami. Driving had become too hectic. A time-consuming chore. Traffic, so much of it on the streets these days...going nowhere.

Traffic was being funneled to the only lane open on the right. Why must traffic always slow down to a halt on both sides of the expressway for an accident?

Nosy people. Either that, or bored.

Time, Xavier understood, equaled money. It was that simple formula this country was founded upon. He remembered his high school history teacher telling the class: "The business of America is making money!"

"Of All The Things I've Lost," read one bumper sticker on the car in front of him, "I Miss My Mind The Most." So many cars. Where was everybody going?

"HE IS HERE!" read another bumper sticker.

The accident up ahead looked serious. A yellow Ryder van had turned on its side and burst into flames. Black smoke mushroomed over the long line of traffic. *When your number comes up, it's time to go.* Thinking of death and dying made Xavier shudder, so to forget about it he reached for his cellular phone and dialed his office number.

It rang three times. The answering machine came on: "You have reached the insurance office of Xavier Cuevas." Darleen, his secretary, sounded scratchy on the tape. She had stepped out for lunch. The machine beeped. He pressed a code number to retrieve the messages. While the machine rewound, he noted the time. He'd been stuck in traffic now for thirty-five minutes. *So many things I need to do*, he thought.

Lately his memory failed. His concentration waned. He constantly wrote little memos to himself to remember things. Sometimes he didn't remember them until Sarah, his wife, showed the crumpled pieces of paper to him before putting his clothes in the washing machine. Was this important? she always asked. By then it was too late, the need to remember specific things had passed. Sarah bought him one of those writing tablets that stick to the windshield and rest on the dashboard.

The machine whirred and clicked. Beeped.

A woman's husky voice came on. She needed quotes on the cheapest auto insurance. "If it's too expensive," she said, "I'll pay only P.I.P."

Xavier wrote *NO MONEY IN IT* on the tablet, then crossed it out.

The next message was a long silence. Xavier waited for a voice to speak, but no one did. Then the line clicked. Somebody'd been doing that a lot lately, calling his number and not leaving messages. Dead silence.

Next on was a client who was unhappy with his group health insurance premiums. The voice sounded familiar, and Xavier tried to figure out who he might be.

The man said, "I am tired of leaving messages. Get back to me, please, or I'm afraid I'll have to take my business someplace else!"

FAMILIAR VOICE.

Another beep.

Then Eloísa, a client from way back when he started to sell insurance, said, "Xavier..." She always pronounced his name with a "J" for *Javier*. "Izquierdo's not well. Not at all." There was a pause during which the faint sound of Eloísa's sobbing became audible. She continued, "*¡De malo a peor!* He wants to see you as soon as you can..." Then she hung up.

Izquierdo was dying of throat cancer from his sixty years of cigar smoking. Xavier made a note to make time to go by. Izquierdo and Eloísa lived in a condo in Kendall, which was in the opposite direction.

The last message was from Xavier's mother.

"*Cariño*," his mother said, "I need to talk to you. Come by if you can."

The machine clicked and whirred and beeped five times, signaling the end of all the messages.

As he returned the phone to its cradle between the front seats, Xavier noticed the driver in a beat-up Ford Pinto making strange gestures at him with his hands. What Xavier had done wrong, he didn't know. The man looked terribly upset; he flipped Xavier the middle finger.

"Same to you buddy," Xavier said.

Once the opportunity opened, the Pinto cut in front of Xavier. The Pinto had New York plates.

Suddenly, the man in the Pinto stepped on the breaks and stopped. Xavier wasn't paying attention and when he realized he was going to crash, he slammed his foot on the break pedal. Then, almost voluntarily, the steering wheel moved under his hands and turned. His car swerved to the right, missing the fender of the Pinto. Xavier drew close enough to see the dents and scratches on the Statue of Liberty plates. *Close call*, he thought, and took a deep breath. His heart beat in his throat. There was a throbbing at his temple.

Up ahead the lights of the police cars, rescue unit and fire truck flashed. Fire fighters doused the flames with a foam spray. Traffic gridlocked.

Finally, when his turn to pass the accident arrived, he turned to look at the foam frothing from the truck's charred and mangled chassis, and then he stepped on the gas. In the rearview mirror he noticed the body covered with a sheet of red plastic. The driver of the truck didn't make it. Hell, driving in this much traffic was too dangerous, but like everyone else, Xavier had to do it.

You take your chances.

Welcome to the hustle and bustle of Miami's daily life.

Northbound on the 826 expressway, getting ready to engage in some heavy-duty cross-lane cutting, Xavier wondered about his mother's call. She sounded worried on the machine. On his way to see a prospective client, he decided to make a pit stop in Hialeah to find out what his mother wanted to talk to him about.

It was twelve minutes past one on a Monday afternoon. Blues Monday. Back-To-The-Grind Monday. He hadn't eaten lunch. His stomach felt hollow. It growled. He'd been on the move since morning, taking care of business. Dropped off a health insurance application, answered calls, checked over the mail-merge list Darleen compiled on the word processor. Pumped gas.

Calls and errands, no time for much else. Such was his life.

Most of his clients were Latinos and often, too often in fact, he couldn't help but feel like an inadequate go-between: an ill-equipped translator between two cultures. You busted your back, he thought, working hard to serve and understand one, *la americanada*, as he called it, and the other, *lo cubiche*, the source of his livelihood, which he protected and respected. *¿Qué es la vida? Caja de sorpresas. Hoy felicidad, mañana tristesa.* These he remembered were the lines of a song by El Gran Combo de Puerto Rico: Life is a box of surprises— today you're happy, tomorrow you're sad.

As soon as he exited the expressway, traffic once again stopped. This time it was for a funeral caravan. A long string of cars with headlights on were escorted by policemen on motorcycles. Traffic stopped at a green light to let all the funeral cars pass. Xavier thought: *They only let you run red lights when you're dead. What good was it then?*

The funeral procession passed and traffic moved again. The phone rang and he picked it up.

"Hey, X," Wilfredo, his office partner, said.

"Where are you?" he asked him.

"Esplain later," Wilfredo said. It bothered Xavier that his partner spoke with such a thick accent when he was capable of speaking without one. They had grown up together, gone to the same schools, learned the same language from the same teachers. Whenever Xavier mentioned the accent, Wilfredo called him an *arrepentido*, embarrassed to be Cuban.

"I've been running around like a chicken with its head chopped off," Xavier said.

Xavier stopped at a red light. "WELCOME TO HIALEAH, The City of the Future," the sign on the median read. Cube City, U.S.A. *Bienvenidos a Hialeah, la ciudad que progresa y tropieza*, the city that progressed and stumbled. This was the city where he had grown up when his family moved here from Cuba in 1960, when he was a year old.

"Monday is not my day," Wilfredo was saying.

"What day of the week is, pal?"

The light turned green and Xavier made a right turn on to 49th Avenue, where the fruit, peanut, newspaper and flower vendors sold their wares in full force, wearing tattered straw hats, weaving among the stopped cars.

"Where are you?" Wilfredo asked.

"On my way to see my mother."

"Say hi to her," Wilfredo said. Then, "You want me to meet you at the office?"

"Don't have the slightest clue when I'll be back." There was a client in Miami Lakes he had to see at two thirty. That gave him enough time to wait out the lunch traffic at his mother's.

A Trans Am sports car with tinted windows cut in front of the Volvo. It was the kind of fast car Wilfredo called a Cuban Ferrari. Wilfredo drove a Camaro, which he called a Cuban Porsche.

"Can't believe this. Fucking traffic!" he said to Wilfredo. "Driving in Hialeah's like entering the Indianapolis 500 on horseback."

Wilfredo laughed.

A short, skinny man approached the Volvo and tapped on the window.

"Hold on," Xavier said.

The instant Xavier rolled down the window, the man slipped in a piece of paper which fell on Xavier's lap. The man walked away quickly. Xavier read the three-by-five index card aloud: "'Phone call, while you were out. Re: personal. Hi, lover; I hear you're an adventurous guy who really likes a good time. Let me make your fantasies come true. Call me. I have a personal message for you...

My number is: 976-3231. Signed, The Foxx.'"

"Save that number," Wilfredo said, and laughed.

Xavier continued, "Two dollars for the first minute, fifty cents for each additional minute. Can you believe it? Some jerk's making money with this crap."

"Sex sells," Wilfredo said. "It's in the constitution."

Xavier tsk-tsked.

"Hey, X," said Wilfredo, his voice full of excitement. Then he switched to Spanish: *"Si vieras la gringa que ligué anoche..."* Xavier should see the Anglo woman Wilfredo picked up last night. "Hot, hot, hot. She's a marine biologist."

Wilfredo was so predictable, or was it because Xavier had known his partner for so long? "A couple of days ago it was an aerobics instructor."

"She told me this incredible story about how octopi mate."

"How *what* mates?"

"Octopus," he said. "Plural for the sea creature with all the *tentáculos*."

"Tentacles, that's the word."

"Listen. The female octopus has her vagina in her nose. If she's not in the mood, you know, and the male tries anything funny, she bites it off."

"Painful stuff."

"Thing is he's got eight penises. Eight tries, then he's out."

"I'd be more careful," he said to Wilfredo, making a note: *All the cars and they all need to be insured.*

"I think I'm in love."

"Same thing you said last week."

"This time it's the real thing."

Xavier fought a strong urge to preach to him about the all too real risks of sleeping around. AIDS lurked behind every smiling face at bars and clubs, places Wilfredo frequented. Wilfredo was playing Russian roulette with five bullets in the barrel.

"Hey, bro, I better let you go," Wilfredo suggested.

Good idea, Xavier thought, then said, "Just about at Mom's."

"See you later, alley gator," Wilfredo told him. "I'm going to have my hands full right now, if you know what I mean."

"Watch out for hernias."

"Noses, *Cubiche*, it's noses I worry about…"

The line clicked.

Xavier hung up and smiled. He couldn't believe his partner's energy—if he only had it for the business.

He turned the corner and pulled up behind his mother's blue Thunderbird in the driveway.

The Hialeah house was in need of paint—rust and mildew had turned the walls orange and green where the spray from the sprinklers hit. How many times had he offered to hire and pay someone to paint the house?

Since his parents' divorce, his mother let the outside of the house go. The lawn needed to be mowed and the hedges trimmed. The roses by the fence dropped their petals and speckled the ground with them.

Before climbing out of the car, Xavier removed his beeper from the sun visor and hooked it to his belt. Switching the vibration buzzer on, he stepped out of the air-conditioned cocoon into the humid, choking heat of the driveway.

Lizards scurried out of the way and hid as Xavier approached the front porch of the house he grew up in. He rang the doorbell but there was no answer. *Should have tried to reach her on the phone before driving out*, he thought. Maybe she had called from work. Perhaps she was on the phone or taking a shower.

His childhood was spent on these streets. He had lost track of how many years his parents had owned the house, having bought it in the early sixties.

The next-door neighbor was sweeping the front steps of her house. She stopped and eyed Xavier. He waved, but the woman continued to sweep.

He rang again, then he heard his mother's footsteps.

Opening the door, she said, "Got my message. Good."

She'd been cleaning. Her hair smelled of detergent and her skin, when he greeted her with a kiss, was moist with perspiration.

"I always get your messages," he said as he entered the house. "I didn't know whether to call you here or at work."

"Took the day off," she said. "Sometimes you've got to do that."

She worked as a buyer for Burdines department store in Westland Mall.

As she led the way to the kitchen, she said, "I don't know why I take days off. I always end up doing work."

"Welcome to the club," he said. "I've been at it since early this morning."

From the rear of the house came the sound of music, a tune Xavier thought he knew because he'd been hearing it most of his life. His mother was playing her old Cuban records, her prized possessions.

Mirna Alarcón was in her late fifties, tall and pretty, though her age showed in the wrinkled skin beneath her almond-colored eyes.

In the kitchen, he could hear the music better; it was the sound of *congas* going *tuc-tuc, tac, tac / truc-truc, truc-trac...*

A wet mop leaned against the refrigerator in the corner of the kitchen. Soapsuds came up in the sink. The Windex and 409 spray bottles sat on top of the stove.

He told her about the impossible traffic and from habit opened the pantry.

"Are you hungry?" his mother asked.

"Hungry's not the word," he admitted, closing the sliding door.

"I ate lunch a while ago," she said. "I can heat up some leftovers."

"I'll pick up something on the way," he said, and sat down on a stool behind the kitchen counter. "I don't want to trouble..."

"Nonsense. Shouldn't eat junk food. All that cholesterol."

He didn't want to ask her pointblank why she had asked him to come over. Obviously she was fine. There was something different about her appearance. It took him a couple of glances to figure it out. A new hair style, cropped short on the sides and bobbed in the back, made her look younger.

"All I have to do," she said, "is heat it up."

She took the Tupperware containers from the refrigerator, spooned the chicken and yellow rice and fried plantain leftovers into a plate, and placed them in the microwave oven.

Since the divorce, his mother tried hard to lead an activity-filled lifestyle. She went on cruises to the Caribbean with her friends. Away to watch the musicals on Broadway. Always came back and talked incessantly about the stuff she saw in New York.

"How..." his mother stopped to press the START button. "How are Sarah and the children?" She sat on the stepladder on the other side of the counter.

"They're fine, mother. Lindy wants to have her ears pierced. She watched how it's done on television."

"Bring her by the store. I'll get someone in Jewelry to pierce them for her," she told him.

"Sarah wants to wait until she's older."

Mirna gave him a look of disapproval, then said, "The longer she waits..." Again she stopped. "And you, how are you doing? How many policies did you sell last week?"

"Not enough."

"*La avaricia rompe el saco*," she said in her clear and soft-spoken Spanish. Avarice corrupts.

"Sink or swim," Xavier told her. "It's the nature of the business. I have to stay afloat or else."

Sink or swim.

That was precisely the way he'd been living for the last few years. Always in a hurry, but never enough time. He felt the tugs and wondered if his time to sink had come.

"I suppose you want to know why I asked you over?" she said.

Xavier flashed her a what-could-be-so-urgent? look.

"I have good news."

At least someone did.

"I wanted to tell you before," she said. "But I had to wait for the right time."

"Did something happen?" he asked, checking the time on the kitchen clock and his watch. He was synchronized.

"Ready?"

"Ready."

"I'm getting married," she said.

He didn't know what to say. He was dumbfounded. *My mother getting married? Why not? But to whom?*

She started to say something but paused. "...Been thinking it over."

"To whom?" he asked. He wondered what kind of expression he had on his face, since his mother was looking at him so strangely.

"This is really difficult for me, *hijo*." She placed a doily in front of him. From the cabinet drawer, she pulled silverware, then she went down into the florida room and turned off the music.

"I am happy for you," he said finally. *Why shouldn't she marry again?* "Who is he?"

"I've always been honest with you, haven't I?" she said from the other room, then returned to the kitchen, set the silverware down in front of him, grabbed a glass from the cupboard and put ice in it.

He agreed.

The food's aroma filled the kitchen with a thick cumin-cilantro-and-chicken-in-yellow-rice smell.

"Well?" he asked.

"Your father and I had lunch the other day. I told him."

"What did he say?" It was news to Xavier that his parents lunched together.

She smiled. "You know how he is." She walked to the microwave to check the food. It was ready. Steam rose from the plate and swirled in front of him. Succumbing to its influence, he felt hungrier than ever.

"Really, what did he say to you? What does he think?" His father was living with a "friend," as Mirna put it, in Miami beach, and Xavier didn't want to think about those living arrangements either.

"There's an avocado," she told him. "I can make you a salad."

Xavier told her not to bother. "Tell me what he said, for Christsakes!"

She got him a Diet Pepsi. She brought him a napkin. The pepper and salt were already on the counter. Xavier missed his mother's attention. Why didn't he come over more often?

"He wished me good luck," his mother said, return- ing to the fold-out step ladder. "He said to me, 'Why spend the rest of your life alone?' So I told him he was absolutely right."

"That's nice of him."

She smiled the way his children smiled when they had a trick up their sleeves or a secret. "Your father's become an understanding man," she said, sarcasm thick in her voice. "We get along fine now that he understands himself better, now that he is—"

"You'll be happy now," Xavier interrupted her.

"Aren't *you* happy for me?" she asked.

"Of course I am."

"I want you to meet him."

"Tell me who he is," he said.

"You'll like him."

"How can I like him if you don't tell me who he is?"

"He styles my hair at the salon."

This caught Xavier off-guard. "Your hairdresser? You are marrying your hairdresser?"

"Hair stylist."

Same thing. He grew quiet. His mood changed and plummeted to murky depths. He put the fork and knife down.

"What's the matter?" she asked.

"I've got to go, mother," he said.

"I thought you were hungry."

"I'm late for an appointment," he lied. He was upset, but he didn't feel like explaining why. Besides, he didn't want to ruin his mother's mood.

It wasn't that he had anything against hairdressers/
stylists. No, it wasn't anything like that. It was the idea
of her getting married. After all these years...

"How about a *cafecito*?" she asked.

"No thanks."

Silence, then she looked at him and said, "Maybe it's
my turn to have a middle-age crisis. You must promise
me not to talk to your father about this."

"I thought you had told him."

"I have," she said, "but I don't want him to talk
behind my back."

"Does he know who you are marrying?"

"It's none of his business."

"You are right," Xavier said, and stood up.

"This man cares about me. Loves me."

His lunch started to sour in his stomach. He went to
the bathroom, washed his hands, splashed cold water on
his face, rinsed his mouth, and combed his hair in front
of the medicine-cabinet mirror. His was a tired face,
tired eyes, and a mouth tired from talking. *Why don't
people ever stop talking?* he wondered as he stared at his
bloodshot eyes. Sometimes he wished he could get by
without speaking.

Mirna's toiletries had taken over the bathroom
completely. There was a bottle of Pierre Cardin mens'
cologne next to the toothbrushes. *Was it his? Probably.
Was he spending nights here?*

What's going to happen to this house? He contemplated. *Would she live here among so many old memories
and make her new marriage work?*

Let her marry who she wanted, it is none of my business. Not mine, nor my father's. It's her happiness. He thought he could make himself understand.

Once again in the kitchen, he thanked his mother for the lunch and congratulated her. *It isn't everyday your mother announces an engagement.*

"Will you be there?" she asked.

"Where?"

"At the wedding."

"When is it?"

"We haven't decided yet, but it'll be soon. Maybe in July."

"Am I invited?"

She hugged and kissed him. "Don't be silly. Who do you think is giving me away?"

Xavier moved to the front door. Mirna followed him there and put her hand on his arm as if to stop him.

She said, "I still care about your father. But I don't want to spend the rest of my life alone."

"You're not alone," Xavier said.

She's an adult, Xavier admitted to himself as a way to form some sort of rationale, *and she has a right to do as she sees fit. But what could she and this man have in common?* He tried to imagine them *sitting around, relaxing, and the man doing her hair all the time. Checking it. Combing it. Fiddling with it. Saying, "I've got to get it perfect. Look at your hair. Your hair's the reason why I married you, darling."*

Xavier realized the unfairness of the stereotype.

"Goodbye, Mother."

"Keep in touch," she said. "I'll send you and Sarah an invitation."

Outside, the harsh midday sunshine made him squint. He got in the car. Putting on his shades, he pulled out of the driveway, waved to his mother, and drove on. He couldn't believe it, his mother getting married, and she wanted him to give her away. He wrote down: *MOTHER'S MARRIAGE.*

Warm air mixed with faint exhaust smells that came out of the Volvo's air vents. He loosened his tie and removed the beeper, hooking it to the usual place on the visor.

DATE?

Twenty minutes to get to Miami Lakes to see his new client. At the corner of 60th Street and 12th Avenue, he made a left and headed westward. School zones in this area slowed down traffic. *No, sir, this city isn't traffic-friendly.* But his appointments had to be kept, calls answered, errands run, and the bills for living paid.

A WEDDING GIFT FOR MOTHER?

Sarah would know what to buy.

He turned the radio on, searched for easy-listening music. Without words. He scanned the stations. No luck. He changed his mind. Turned off the radio. *Silence is more gratifying.*

Xavier leaned his head back against the headrest. A tension headache started behind his eyes, heartburn in his chest.

Back in traffic, Xavier Cuevas was on the move again.

Sometimes in the insurance business, Xavier knew, a name and an address are enough to draw some preliminary conclusions about a prospective client. The following information, written on a 3M adhesive note paper, stuck to the outside of a folder: Octavio Segovia. Age: 39. Address: 1414 Lake Front Drive, Miami Lakes.

Señor Segovia had called the office and in a rather young, clear voice wanted to know about life insurance premiums. Xavier supposed the man to be a family man, like most of his life insurance clients, and concerned about the welfare of his family in case of a premature death. The address belonged to an affluent neighborhood in Miami Lakes.

Fourteen-fourteen stood at the end of the curving street, across from a school playground. It was a two-story house with a blue tile roof. A wrought-iron balcony ran along its front and side above a three-car garage. Bougainvillea grew next to it.

Xavier drove up to the intercom. He composed himself, combed his hair and straightened his tie. First impressions, he had learned, were as important as smooth talk and sales know-how. He looked up at the surveillance camera.

His headache still pulsed, but it had lost its rough edge the minute he stopped thinking about his mother getting married. The stomach ache lingered, making him self-conscious. A belch rose in his throat.

Gas, he thought, *that's all I need.*

Quickly, he pondered over the life insurance packages and premiums and prepared a sales strategy. Selling insurance was like playing soccer. You hustled the
ball up field, faked the goalie, and kicked in the winning
goal.

Xavier, the sharpshooter.

The static-filled voice from the speaker asked for
identification. The camera turned to face him.

"I have a two-thirty appointment to see Mr. Segovia," he shouted.

"Your name?" asked a voice with a thick Central
American accent.

Xavier looked up at the camera and said his name.

"Javier?"

"No, with an X. *X*avier."

"Listen carefully to the following instructions," the
voice said. "When the gate opens, drive around the circular driveway and park in the second space to your left.
Please wait inside your car. Somebody will be there to
greet you."

There was a moment of silence.

"Do you understand?" the voice asked.

"Loud and clear," Xavier projected up into the intercom box.

The speaker clicked off. The iron gate slid open.
Xavier drove in and followed directions.

In the center of the circular driveway was a fountain: three lions with open mouths from which water
flowed in graceful arcs.

Xavier parked the car next to a shiny black, convert-
ible Jaguar XJ-S with tinted windows, bronze chrome

work on the fenders and spoked wheel rims. The plate read: SEGOVIA. On the other side sat an emerald Mercedes Benz and a white limousine.

A man dressed in a gray, three-piece suit and wearing sunglasses waited nearby. *In this heat...he must be crazy*, Xavier thought. Gesturing for Xavier to turn off the engine, the man approached Xavier's Volvo on the driver's side.

"Step out of the car, please," the man said.

Removing his seat belt, Xavier looked at the short, dark-skinned man. A receding hair line left an obvious difference in skin color between the man's forehead and scalp.

As Xavier stepped out of the car he pulled his briefcase behind him. The man, eyes hidden behind sunglasses, asked Xavier to place the briefcase on the hood of his car.

"Please open it," he said.

The man searched through the partitions in the briefcase, checked under the manila folders and files. He picked up the calculator, removed the battery compartment lid and took the batteries out. He stared down the hollow chamber, then put the batteries back in, sealed them with the lid and returned the calculator to the briefcase.

The man finished inspecting the briefcase, closed it, and then reached for Xavier's chest. "Please put your arms out," the man said as if he were asking to shake hands. He felt down the sides of Xavier's chest and waist. Finally the man was through with his search. "Please follow me," he said, and headed inside the house.

It was huge. *Would I be found if I got lost in here?* Xavier wondered as he entered the cool air-conditioned foyer.

A loud "Squaaaaaaak!" startled him.

He turned to find a bird preening its blue-red feathers atop a huge wrought-iron cage. A macaw. The bird stopped moving and eyed the intruder.

"Nice bird," Xavier told the man.

"SQUAAAAAAAAAAAAAAAAACK!" cried the bird.

"Don Octavio will be with you shortly," the man said, and took his place by the door. "Have a seat."

The living room was filled with nude female sculptures and abstract paintings. Ferns hung everywhere. In the middle of the room was a circular, white-fabric sofa and in the center, on a round glass table, sat a red globe that looked like a big tomato. Xavier sat down on the sofa facing the man and the door. The sofa was as cushiony as a water bed. *How much money must flow into Segovia's hands? How easily? From where?* He placed the briefcase on his lap and opened it. The clicking of the locks attracted the security guard's attention.

Pretending to be busy, Xavier fingered through some of the files as he waited for Segovia to appear.

The instant Segovia made his entrance, he smiled as if he'd known the insurance salesman all his life. Not much taller than five-nine, Segovia's slimness made him look taller. They shook hands. He had a strong grip.

"Señor Cuevas," Segovia said, friendliness gleaming in his brown eyes.

"Call me Xavier."

"I appreciate you coming out this far to see me."

"No trouble at all," Xavier said.

Segovia's arms and forearms were tanned under his white short-sleeved *guayabera*. Taking a seat next to Xavier, Segovia asked, "Would you like a drink? A cocktail?"

"No, thank you," Xavier said. "Nice place you have here."

"I designed it," said Segovia. "It took me a while to find the right lot, but once I did, the rest was easy."

There was an uncomfortable pause. Finally, Xavier began his pitch. "Since you called, I've prepared two life packages. I think you'll be very interested in them."

Segovia leaned back into the sofa and crossed his legs.

"The Whole Life Plan accumulates more equity than regular life. You pay a fixed amount, then after that it pays itself."

Mr. Segovia lifted his hand from his knee and gestured for Xavier to stop.

"Forgive my ignorance," Segovia admitted, "but let me tell you what I want. Then you can look for the best way to accommodate me. Okay?"

Xavier regained his composure and turned to listen. He was having a hard time making himself comfortable. Again, he felt like belching. "By all means," Xavier agreed.

"What's the highest amount I can be insured for?"

"Ten million," Xavier answered automatically.

Segovia pondered the figure, then continued, "That's the amount my beneficiaries receive in case of my?..."

"Death. Exactly."

"And the premiums?"

"Monthly?"

"Yes, monthly," he said.

"Two-thousand dollars."

"Can I pay in cash?"

"Whatever's most convenient. All you have to do is sign the application," Xavier said, handing the form to Mr. Segovia.

Segovia found the places marked with an X and signed.

"I'll fill in the rest," Xavier assured him.

"I want to make sure," Segovia told him, "my children don't have to struggle the way I did."

"I understand."

Segovia drew a roll of one-hundred dollar bills from his pocket and counted six thousand, placing the bills between him and Xavier. Segovia's hands and fingers looked rough, but manicured. The cut cuticles exposed the perfect half moons of his nails.

He said, "This should be enough for the first quarter, right?"

"Absolutely." Xavier thought. *I'll put it all in the bank and turn in two thousand per month. Let the other four gain interest.*

Xavier stacked the bills, put a rubber band around them and placed them inside the folder with the signed forms. He returned the folder and locked the briefcase.

"It's been a pleasure," Segovia said, standing.

They shook hands and Segovia signaled to the man by the door to show Xavier the way back to the car.

Xavier told Segovia not to hesitate, to call the office if he had any questions.

"Never hesitate," Segovia said.

As the guard escorted Xavier past the macaw, it tried to peck Xavier's arm. At Xavier's Volvo, the man waited for him to get in, start the car, and drive out.

Xavier checked the time. In and out, that's the way he liked to conduct business. *Not bad at all*, he said to himself and tapped the surface of the briefcase. On the notepad, he jotted down: TOMORROW MAKE FOL-LOW-UP CALL. SEND A COPY OF THE AP & RECEIPT.

Boys played soccer out on the field now. One kicked the ball over the fence. Xavier stopped the car, backed up, got out of the car and fetched the ball.

"Hey, dude," said one of the boys, "throw it back."

Xavier held the ball in his hand—it was official size and weight. It had been a long time since he'd held a soccer ball.

"Over here," shouted the goalie. A couple of other players waved.

Xavier threw them the ball, but it fell short and hit the top of the fence. It bounced back on the side of the street and landed on the grassy edge of the sidewalk.

He walked over to the ball and picked it up.

"Kick it!"

Then, Xavier took a few steps forward and kicked the ball as hard as he could with the leg with which he could still kick. The ball went high over the fence but away from the boys.

They laughed at his weak effort and lack of general aim as they ran over to the edge of the fence to get their ball back.

"Punks," Xavier said loud enough to be heard, but they didn't seem to care. For them, he thought, he was an old man.

Xavier dusted his hands off and got back in the car.

It was still early enough for him to go to the office, check up on things, then home. Early enough indeed to try and beat the rush-hour traffic.

Wishful thinking. Heavy traffic awaited him southbound on the 836 expressway near the airport. A traffic update said there were two accidents on I-95 and a stalled vehicle up ahead on the 836. Xavier resigned himself to wait. This was the way it was every day. He'd gotten used to it.

The telephone rang. It was his daughter Lindy. She wanted to know when he was getting home.

"Gotta go by the office first, sweetheart," Xavier told her, holding the phone away from his ear because his five-year-old tended to shout.

"Where are you?"

"Stuck in traffic," he said, "but I'll be home soon."

Then Lindy screamed and dropped the phone.

"Hey, Lindy!" he said.

"Know what, Dad?" shouted Eric on the phone now.

Lindy cried in the background.

"You didn't hit your sister, did you, Eric?"

"She's a crybaby, Dad."

"Eric!"

"Mom took us to the pet shop," he said.

"Put your mother on."

"She's in the bathroom," lisped his son.

"Tell her I'll be home soon."

"She wants to talk to you."

"Give her the phone."

"I told you, Dad, she's in the bathroom. She's singing. Go get Mom, Lindy!"

Singing? In the bathroom?

"Mom bought us fighting fish."

"She did?" Xavier wondered what a fighting fish was.

"Mine is bigger," Eric told his sister.

"No it isn't," Lindy shouted in the background. Lindy stopped crying.

"It's got purple and red fins. I'm holding it in my hand."

"In your hand?" Xavier asked, believing anything from Eric.

"Lindy got one, too. Mine's bigger. Their real names are Bettas."

"Get your mother, Eric."

"Dad, I'm going to put the fish together. Let them fight."

Lindy: "NO, WE ARE NOT!"

"Son, put your mom on."

"YES, WE ARE! I want to see them fight," he said, delighted at the idea.

Xavier heard Lindy struggling to get the phone back. He pictured Eric holding his sister back with his free arm.

"Hey, Dad..."

"What, Eric?"

"You coming home now? You gotta see..."

Sarah came on.

"Don't let the kids fight," he said.

"They are not fighting now," she answered. Hers was the voice of understanding motherhood—if it was all right with the kids, then it was okay with her, too.

Xavier told her that he was on the way home.

"Good," she said. "I need you to pick up a dress from the dry cleaners."

"Which one?"

"Which dress?"

"No, which cleaners?" he asked.

"The one on the corner of Ponce and Eighth Street."

"Don't let Eric pick on his sister."

"The bill's paid. Don't forget to pick it up."

"I'll try."

"When do you think you'll be home?" she asked.

"Soon as I get out of this traffic, go by the office, and pick up your dress."

"Later," she said, and hung up.

If she only knew that I am trying to go faster, he thought, *but can only go so fast. What good is speed when I am stuck in traffic? If I pick up the pace, who knows where I'd go? Nothing, he figured, nothing can slow me down, nothing but this fucking traffic.*

The office was on the third floor of a bank building off Miracle Mile, in the heart of Coral Gables. Suite 305. An office with three rooms, one for Wilfredo and the larger one for Xavier. Also, a reception area where Darleen had her desk and a computer work table. No windows, but the wall of mirrors facing the entrance made the place seem larger.

Xavier stopped at the office to drop off Segovia's application. Wilfredo could process it at the main office in the morning. He also wanted to leave Darleen tomorrow's work schedule.

Neither Wilfredo nor Darleen were in the office now. Unopened mail rested on Wilfredo's desk. Darleen had gone home for the day.

It was almost five-thirty. Xavier sat behind his heavy oak desk and contemplated all the work yet to be done. Darleen left several phone messages clipped to one corner of the calendar: nine messages scribbled in her tiny print. The last one he read was from his father. Carlos Antonio called him from work at four-thirty.

Then there was a stack of cancelled policies that needed to be reinstated—Wilfredo could have done all this. Frustrated, Xavier dialed, but the line in Wilfredo's apartment was busy. *Probably planning another outing for tonight*, Xavier thought. Wilfredo refused to get a beeper, but it was becoming clear that he'd have to carry one.

From the top right-hand drawer of the desk he removed a yellow-lined writing tablet and on it wrote a list of things for Darleen to do when she came in at nine o'clock. He jotted down this short note to leave on Wilfredo's desk:

WIL, SEE ME SOME TIME THIS YEAR. WE NEED TO TALK!

Then he put all of Segovia's cash, except for two grand, in an envelope for Darleen to take to the bank, and filled out a deposit slip. He placed the envelope and the rest of the cash in the safe under the credenza. Xavier added to Darleen's list instructions on what to do with the money.

Dialing his business partner's phone number once more, he realized that he only had fifteen minutes to make it to the cleaners to pick up Sarah's dress before the place closed. The line was still busy.

One look at the clock told him that if he didn't hurry, he wasn't going to make it to the cleaners. Today felt like the longest day of his life. Mostly he felt drained. Exhausted. All that time in the car...

He left the office, drove in the heavy Calle Ocho traffic to the cleaners and found it closed.

"Shit," he said as he got out of the car and approached the tinted front door from where the SORRY WE'RE CLOSED sign hung. He put his face to the glass, but couldn't see anybody behind the front counter. He tapped on the glass with his wedding band. No one came.

Sarah would have to live without her dress one more day. Anyway, she had a closet full of clothes. Let her come up with a solution to her dilemma.

Home was on Arabia Street in Coral Gables: a white Mediterranean with red roof tiles, three bedrooms, and two and a half bathrooms. This was the house Carlos Antonio bought after his divorce from Mirna. When he started developing properties in Miami Beach, he decided to move closer to work. Without the break from his father, Xavier and Sarah couldn't afford to live in this part of the city.

Xavier parked next to Sarah's gray Honda Civic. Eric's skateboard and Lindy's hot-pink bicycle blocked the stairs at the entrance to the porch. The front door was wide open. When he entered the house, he found it empty.

"Anybody home?" he called out. *Somebody forgot to close the front door.*

He received no answer.

Xavier couldn't help but worry that one day someone would walk in and rob them, or worse, kill everybody. He grew angry, but he'd had a tough day and he was determined to relax. In the kitchen, Xavier placed his briefcase on the counter, unbuttoned his shirt, and got some water out of the refrigerator.

The phone rang and he picked it up.

"Hello?" said a woman. "Is Mrs. Triste there?"

Triste was Sarah's maiden name.

"This is her husband," he said, and took a drink of water.

"Will you please tell her to call Mary at Holiday Travel regarding her flight information?"

"Okay."

"Thank you. Goodbye."

He hung up, drank the rest of the water, then returned the empty glass to the sink.

Brandy, the toy fox terrier, should have greeted him by now. Where was everybody? When he heard Brandy bark, he looked out the kitchen window. Everyone was out beyond the patio deck, the kids kneeling on the dirt as Sarah stood behind them. Xavier walked out of the house and onto the deck.

Brandy ran over when she saw her master. Wagging her tail, she circled his legs. Sarah looked up at him, but didn't say anything. Eric and Lindy kept their eyes closed, hands together in prayer.

"What's going on, guys?" he asked.

Sarah, dressed in a backless summer dress, approached him. She was tall, even when barefoot. In the sun her blonde hair and green eyes made her striking. He found solace in her all-American good looks, including her broad smile of perfect teeth.

The kids, with their blond hair and fair skin, looked like her and nothing like him.

"Did you pick up the dress?" she asked, squinting up at him.

"Place closed."

"You forgot," she said. She put her hand on her forehead to keep the sun out of her eyes.

"I didn't forget," he said. "The place closed before I got there."

She looked at him long and hard. "Never mind."

"I went by."

"Forget it."

"It's been a tough day," he said.

"A simple favor."

"Damn place closed. What did you want me to do? Break in?"

"I said forget it."

"Look," he said, "next time you run your own errands."

"Let's drop it, okay?"

Xavier looked at the kids. "What are you guys doing?"

"Dad," Eric said, fighting back his tears, "Lindy's fish killed mine."

"We buried it here," Lindy said, and tapped on the little grave with her black and white polka-dot Keds.

"Watch the cross, honey," Sarah told her.

A tiny cross, made out of two glued popsicle sticks, was stuck in the mound of dirt.

Xavier moved closer to Eric and Lindy to greet them with a hug and a kiss, but Eric no longer liked to be kissed and Lindy wanted to be carried piggyback.

"Dad, my fish died," Eric said. "She killed it."

"No, I didn't," said Lindy, saddened and sorry about the whole ordeal.

"Don't worry, Eric," Xavier told his son, "we'll get you another fish."

"Another fighting fish, Dad?"

"No, not unless you promise not to make them fight," warned Sarah on her way to the kitchen door.

"I promise," Eric said.

Xavier picked up Lindy and carried her inside. She was still light enough to be carried. She smelled faintly of Playdough. Lindy showed her father the colorful fish in the bowl which sat on the kitchen window sill.

"Mary at Holiday Travel called," he said to Sarah in the kitchen.

"Can I take your briefcase, Daddy?" his daughter asked.

"Thank you, baby." He put his daughter down.

"What did she want?" asked Sarah.

"Something about flight information."

"I don't need it anymore," she said. An instant of silence rose between them. "Someone at work needs to fly," she continued. Sarah worked as program director for the Miami Opera Guild.

"Your mother called," she said.

"I saw her today."

"She wants me to take Lindy by the store to pierce her ears."

"TV time!" Eric said.

"Give her a call."

"She also said to ask you about the good news."

"Later," he said. He didn't feel like talking about his mother getting married.

For a moment he stood in the fluorescent brightness of the kitchen, among the appliances and boxes and jars and potted plants on the window sill, next to the fish and the finger paintings stuck with magnets to the refrigerator door. He watched Lindy as she dragged the briefcase across the dining room floor and heaved it on top of a chair by the glass cabinet.

"What's for dinner?" Xavier asked.

"The kids want pizza," said Sarah.

"Yeah, pizza," Lindy said from the living room. "LET'S GO TO CHUCK E. CHEESE'S!"

"McDONALD'S!" Eric shouted from the foot of the stairs.

"We're eating in," said Sarah, and got on the phone to Dominos pizza and was put on hold.

"I'm going up to take a bath," Xavier said, and left her standing in the kitchen.

He climbed the stairs and went to the master bedroom, removed his clothes and entered the bathroom. He sighed at his nakedness. His muscles looked limp. Having little time, he'd been away from exercise too long. It showed, especially on his flabby, pale chest. When flexed, his pectorals no longer possessed any firmness. *This is not my body*, he thought. *Certainly not the body of my youth.* It felt strange and unfamiliar. The only strong muscles were on his thighs. *Powerful legs all right.* But the scars on his right knee reminded him of some painful memories, which he now tried hard not to recall. *Do not look at those thick scars.* He turned away from the mirror.

Several of Sarah's old music books stuck out in the magazine rack. He remembered Eric mentioning something about Sarah singing in the bathroom. *She must have been practicing, reliving her moments as an opera singer.*

Xavier felt his tension headache return, so he grabbed the bottle of extra-strength Tylenols out of the medicine cabinet, twisted the cap off, and shook a couple of pills onto his hand. He popped them in his mouth and swallowed. *Old routines die hard.* Then he opened the faucet in the tub and let the water run until steam filled the bathroom. Xavier stepped into the tub and sat down. He leaned back slowly, letting the heat envelop him. *This should do it.*

Trying hard to relax, he attempted to forget about work, his family, his mother marrying a hairdresser, his irresponsible business partner, but he didn't succeed.

After the pizza dinner and a little family interaction—the kids watched TV and Sarah, still upset about her dress, kept out of sight in other rooms—Xavier turned in early. He thought he could get some sleep, but sleep never comes easily for those who need it most. Tonight Xavier needed it desperately. He tossed and turned, trying to find a comfortable position. After Sarah made the kids wash up and get in bed, she came to bed, still not saying anything. She went into the bathroom and when she came out, she climbed into bed and went to sleep.

Xavier thought in the darkness, sighing often. He thought of his kids sleeping in the other room. Of Sarah here next to him. Sound asleep. Her breathing quiet, rhythmic. *If only it were contagious.* Maybe the pizza they'd eaten for dinner didn't agree with his stomach.

A prickling sensation started at his feet and worked its way up his legs. The room was too hot; the air too heavy. He heard the soft buzzing of the radio/alarm clock, the static Z sound. *Or was it Sarah's breathing?* Dogs barked in faraway yards. Trying not to wake up Sarah, he turned to look at the time. It was thirty-one minutes past midnight.

From the airport came the roar of planes taking off. *People on the move, going places, arriving, meeting more people. Such hectic moments.*

Then he thought about Wilfredo. What was that rascal up to right now? Probably at a night club, quickly on his way to getting smashed. *Pedo*, as Wilfredo called it. They'd come a long way from those high school days. There was a time when Wilfredo was not only his best friend, but a confidant. They'd spend nights drinking beer in the car, parked behind the football field, shootin' the breeze and making sense of what Xavier should do about his troubles at home. After Xavier received his AA degree at Miami Dade Community College, Wilfredo advised him to go away to school, accept the soccer scholarship to the University of Arizona.

It was either that or wait to be drafted if the United States invaded Iran to get those hostages out. Ronald Reagan was about to take over the White House from Jimmy Carter.

Xavier liked being in the desert. Being far from Miami gave him a new perspective on what to do with his life. He wanted to become a professional soccer player. Back when he was an All-Star forward for the Pioneers at North Miami High School and then at Miami Dade Community College, he had all the attention, but in Tucson, he was merely another good player.

What happened to the last decade? There really wasn't a beginning, middle, or end to these last ten years. Back in the tenth grade, if someone would have said to me, "Xavier, ten years from now you will be selling insurance, have your own office, be married, have two kids," I'd have laughed so hard and said no, not me, no way.

Every day passed the same way, full of trivial errands. The system was set up like that. You could tell what day of the week it was by listening to the radio. Monday was "Blues Monday." You hated to have to go back to work, but you had to because the bills *had* to be paid. Tuesday, "Double-Shot Tuesday," meaning you heard two songs by the same artist played on the radio, or went to a bar to drink two shots of liquor for the price of one. Wednesday was "Hump Day." Middle of the week. Thursday you started to get ready for the weekend, and if you went out to the clubs, the way Wilfredo did, then it was "Ladys' Night Out." Friday was "Thank God It's Friday." Lots of happy hours and parties going on, but not when you had to run an office. Then the weekend arrived. If lucky, you got up no earlier than eight. By then the kids had already eaten breakfast and were playing outside. Sarah was reading the newspaper and planning her day. Sunday you rested unless there were loose ends, and there were always those. Then it was over. Weekends zoomed by and the whole process started up again. It was all the same, day in, day out, week in, week out...the years piling up.

The last ten years ran away from him like horses spooked by thunder.

When he closed his eyes he could hear the loud snap of his right knee giving out. The pain immediately took him down. He remembered the team doctor probing the knee, and the pain, ah, that excruciating pain! It felt like a red-hot railroad spike piercing the skin and breaking through the bone. They carried him off the field on a stretcher. No standing ovation.

Why am I feeling sorry for myself? He needed to stop thinking about his past. All the possibilities of what might have been. The death of his aspirations.

Next thing he knew he found himself in the locker room with the doctor wrapping ice packs around his knee, saying, "Doesn't look good, X. We'll see what the x-rays show, but it won't be good."

The doctor was right; he was never able to play again, even after two corrective surgeries.

But Sarah, with whom he lived, saved him from self-destruction, didn't she?

Turning over on his side, he woke up Sarah.

"What's wrong?" she asked.

"Nothing."

"Turn yourself off for the night," she said, then turned away from him and fell right back to sleep.

Not that easy.

It was the end of his second year at Miami Dade Community College and he had already been offered the scholarship to go to Tucson. The Wildcats didn't have the best soccer team, but the scholarship money tempted Xavier enough to accept. Besides, by then he wanted to get as far away from his parents as possible.

After he got the scholarship toward the end of the summer, Xavier remained in town long enough to pack and say goodbye to his friends.

Then one Saturday morning, Xavier loaded up his Mustang, took the turnpike and headed north to Interstate 75, then west on I-10. On the road map he saw there was no way for him to get lost. He drove straight, only stopping for food, gas, and a couple of hours of sleep in the rest areas. The trip took two days and two nights. He crossed most of Texas by night.

By the third day he found himself in Tucson. There he was. In prickly pear and saguaro cactus country. Sand and pebbles as shiny as mother-of-pearl buttons. Rocks, boulders, mountains, canyons, strange looking lizards and rodents—America as he had never seen it. On the way to the foothills he stopped for a late lunch at a Denny's. He asked the waitress if she knew of any places for rent in the vicinity, having figured out that it would be cheaper not to stay in the school dorms. He'd have more freedom, too.

"Look in the university paper," she said. Then, "But you better hurry, the place's swarming. Parents everywhere looking for good deals for their kids."

He left the waitress a tip, paid the check at the register, and set out to find a place to live. He'd check in with the athletic department office later, tell them their shotgun kid had arrived.

In the university paper, he found a place for rent, cheap and not too far from the stadium side of campus. He looked up the address on a map of Tucson he'd bought at a gas station where he'd stopped for gas. Once there, he parked and scrutinized the place. The adobe house stood behind a couple of mesquite bushes and a weathered picket fence. The name *S. Triste* was painted with red nail polish on the lid of the mailbox.

He stood on the porch's dusty floor boards, opened the torn screen door and knocked. At first he heard nothing, then a young woman opened the door and smiled at him.

"Place still for rent?" he asked.

"Oh, yeah," she said, "sure, come on in."

"Cuevas," he introduced himself, "Xavier Cuevas."

"Not *Javier*?"

"No, with an X."

She showed him the place.

"I like old houses," he said.

Sarah showed him the rest of the house, pointing out what could or couldn't be fixed. "The owner lives in Phoenix," she said. "He only comes to Tucson once in a blue moon." *Once in a blue moon...* By then he was too far gone on her voice, her expressions, the way she kept pushing her long blonde hair over one ear; he could have cared less about the cracks on the bedroom walls or the leak stains on the ceilings.

In the spare room, which she used as a study, and which would be his room, paint had sealed the windows shut.

"I'll get all my stuff out of the way," she said.

"Don't worry about it," he assured her. "I didn't bring too much with me."

"A light traveler."

He smiled.

"Are you a student?" she asked in the bathroom, her voice a soft whisper among the broken tiles and leaky faucets.

"Soccer," he told her. "Left Miami and came here to play."

"An athlete."

Xavier asked, "What do you do?"

"Sing opera," she said as she led him back to the living room. "I'm a voice major. Getting my Bachelors in two more semesters."

"I like this place," he told her as he walked back toward the living room.

She went over the money arrangements slowly. Xavier wrote her a check and then left her standing on the porch as he went to get his stuff out of the car.

Sunset after sunset he sat on the rotting porch steps and watched the sky blaze. In the desert the night came about slowly, stealthily, bringing with it the noises of the

crickets to replace that of the cicadas. The wind sifted
through the dry foliage. From inside the house, the
sounds of Sarah playing her flute, long, pipey whistles,
charmed Xavier. When it wasn't the flute, it was her
singing. For hours, she practiced and rehearsed.

Usually he sat there and while she sang he visual-
ized the scrimmages and drills, sometimes matching his
moves to the rhythm of her singing. Even on the practice
field at the University he imagined her singing. The
openness and air of the desert felt wonderful, boosting
his energies. Mr. Hoyos, the Mexican-American coach,
took a liking to him. Liked him but drilled him hard,
pushed him to the limits. Xavier's footwork improved.
There was a ninety percent chance that he'd be one of
the starting forwards for the Wildcats. "Los Gatos," as
the coach called the team.

During those first weeks, he got to know Sarah well.
She helped him type his papers for school. Sometimes
she put on a classical record (Bach, Mozart, Beethoven),
walked out of the house and joined him on the porch.

"Missed it," he said. "A hawk landed on that mesquite." He pointed to the tree by the fence. "It sat there
and cleaned its beak on the wood."

She asked him questions about Miami. It was one of
the cities on her list to explore after graduation. One of
her voice teachers was moving there. Miami had a growing opera scene. She would teach to support herself,
until she landed a part. Often, she talked about the dog-
eat-dog competition for roles in New York's opera scene,
and how getting one without an agent was next to

impossible. "Sometimes it's not how good you are," she said, "but who you know."

Jogging one night, he raced her back to the house and she beat him because he fell and scraped his leg. A bad slide. He kicked strongest with that leg; it was his shotgun. The graze burned like crazy. She helped him up and into the house and sat him on the sofa, left the living room, and returned with a first-aid kit.

"This is going to hurt," she said.

With a gauze pad, she cleaned the bruise with hydrogen peroxide. It tingled. Then she applied iodine and it burned. Sarah's face drew close to his. He put his hands on her face and kissed her. She took Xavier by the hand and led him to her bed.

"Go slow," he said.

"This," said she, climbing on top of him, "should heal you."

During that time of the night when things always seemed to go wrong, Xavier got out of bed. He grabbed his robe from behind the bedroom door hook and put it on as he hurried downstairs. Brandy woke up. She waited in the dining room, expecting Xavier to take her outside.

He picked up the kitchen phone and dialed his father's number in an urgent need to hear Carlos Antonio's voice. He let the phone ring several times, then hung up, feeling guilty for not staying on and giving his father a chance to answer.

What's the matter, son? Xavier imagined his father asking him.

Can a man ever change his life?

Sure. I did it.

I don't mean that way.

How do you mean?

Can a man walk away and forget it all?

That would be cowardly.

Even if he is on a collision course?

Even so.

I've bitten a big chunk, Dad. More than I can chew.

Everybody's got problems.

These are mine.

Don't let responsibilities get the best...

Brandy barked.

Xavier's chest tightened. The shivers gave him goose bumps. Hot flashes. A cold sweat.

Brandy sat on her haunches by the doorway and whimpered.

He dialed again and let the phone ring and ring and ring. His father wasn't home, so he hung up. Xavier opened the kitchen door and let the dog out. He followed her to the patio. She ran to the usual spot by the fence, sniffed around, then squatted.

It was hot and humid out. A fine mist lingered in the air over everything. Out here was frog heaven. Their cacophonous calls and croaks rose from the banks of the canal. Whenever he had trouble falling asleep, he came out here and sat down on one of the patio chairs. The mosquitos didn't bother him much. *Maybe they don't like my blood*, he thought, embittered by too much worry.

Brandy spotted a frog and started to bark. Xavier walked over, caught the frog, and threw it into the canal. The frog plopped like a stone breaking the surface.

Frogs emerged from the canal banks to hunt for the moths and bugs that swarmed around the patio spot lights. Xavier hated frogs, always had, and didn't know exactly why. One summer during a week of ceaseless rain, he caught sixty-three frogs. Perhaps he despised them because in addition to the rain, they were the constant that you could count on in tropical places.

Everything merged into the darkness. Brandy, by the fence, kept guard over the darkness. *What did she sense? What could be out there hiding? Frogs*, he figured, *more wide-eyed frogs keeping vigil. Maybe ducks. Maybe alligators. Maybe snakes.*

Plenty of mosquitos.

When they first moved into the house, Xavier thought of rowing for exercise or going for walks with the children on the street side of the canal, across the bridge. Could. Didn't. The canal reminded him he couldn't do the things he wanted. He didn't have enough time.

The canal also bred alligators and water moccasins, but they never came into the fenced-in yard. Xavier read stories in the paper of people's dogs disappearing at night.

A loud cracking noise startled him. Brandy snarled and barked at the bushes. Something that Brandy sensed and barked at hid in the dark.

Xavier picked her up and took her inside. From a box on top of the refrigerator he grabbed one of her doggy treats and dropped it in front of her. He felt edgy. The night air didn't help him any.

He thought of calling his father again, but changed his mind. He'd try again in the morning when, if he couldn't reach his father at home, he'd call him at the office.

Brandy followed her master all the way to the stairway, then Xavier patted her goodnight and turned off the lights. Upstairs the kids were sound asleep. Lindy, under her Barbie comforter, slept peacefully on her white oak bed; Eric, one leg hanging over the side of his bed, snored. Xavier reached over and placed his son's leg back on the mattress and then tucked him in. Xavier stood there motionless, as if to absorb all the silence. The glow-in-the-dark lampshade next to the kids' beds reminded Xavier of B-movie radioactivity.

How many sleepless nights had he sat here in the dark and watched his children sleep?

Back in the bedroom, Xavier removed his robe and climbed in bed.

Sarah rolled over. He could sense that she was awake, even though her eyes were closed.

"Everything's fine," he said under his breath. *Tomorrow is another day*, he mused. *No, today. In a matter of hours the alarm will go off. In a few hours...* he clasped his hands behind his head and closed his eyes. He felt drained enough now to fall asleep. Tired enough not to have the kind of anxiety-driven dreams that made him wake in a cold sweat in the middle of the night.

When Xavier entered his office the morning after the sleepless night, bad news was there to greet him. Darleen—her face gone soft and pudgy around her cheeks and chin, dressed in an ankle-long flower-pattern skirt and a canary-yellow cotton-knit blouse, stood in front of his desk and explained to him what had happened.

"I was here at eight. Hoot, I think maybe a little earlier," she said in a thick Southern accent. "First thing I did was read the things-to-do-today list."

Xavier noticed she wasn't quite looking into his eyes. She stared at some other part of his face, perhaps his ears. Hair? More of it turning gray.

"I read it," she continued, "and got some of the easier tasks out of the way, you know, before the bank opened.

"When it was time, I went to the safe, knelt, and turned the combination on the lock, opened the lid, and removed the money. I put the bills in my purse. I also checked the deposit slip.

"I decided to walk instead of drive there. Everything's fine and dandy, then the two men come out of nowhere," Darleen said.

Out of nowhere, this was the part Xavier couldn't understand. He looked at her, then said, "They must have been *somewhere*, Darleen. People don't pop up from thin air."

"Oh, I know, I know," she admitted. Perspiration collected over her make-up.

She spoke slowly: "The two men were Hispanic—one was dark-skinned like Wilfredo, and the other one was white like me. They spoke Spanish, so I couldn't understand what they were saying. I thought they were asking me for directions, or the time or something. I didn't know."

DARK / WHITE / SPANISH, Xavier tried to jot down on a legal pad the most important details, but of course, he wasn't concentrating—all he thought about was Segovia's money.

"The dark one grabbed me from behind. Put me in a headlock..."

"Why didn't you call me right away?" he asked.

"Wait, let me finish, please. I'll get to that. Anyway, he put me in a headlock. Real hard. Choking me."

"Weren't there people walking by?" he asked.

"No, not when the men attacked me," she said, "but some people rushed out of the bank when I screamed."

"Out of the bank?"

"Yes, out of the bank. I was only twenty feet from the entrance."

Darleen's eye shadow streaked as her eyes became moist.

"While one grabbed me by the neck, the other yanked my purse away. Yanked and pulled so hard my arm's still hurting."

"We'll get a doctor to look at it," Xavier said.

"Soon as they had my purse," continued Darleen, "they...they smelled bad."

"Like what?" he asked, and wrote down: *SMELL?*

"Something raunchy."

"You mean rancid."

"No, raunchy, like dirty clothes," she said.

There was a pause here during which Xavier reached over for his no-spill coffee mug and noticed how his hand trembled. Sipping the coffee, he realized that it was cold. Yesterday's coffee. His fingers shook as though they each had a nervous system of their own. Xavier dropped his hands to his lap under the desk and held them there.

"They took off running. One after the other. Both men turned at the corner, and by then I was screaming my lungs out. Only then did people come out of the bank to find out what was happening."

"You should have called me," he said.

"I wanted to, after everything happened. But I was so nervous, you know, the kind of nerves that make your stomach jump. I couldn't remember neither the number at your house or your beeper."

"Where was the bank security?"

"Oh," she said, "he came later."

This was taking too much of his energy.

"He was the one who called the police," she said.

"What did *they* do?"

"They wrote a report. I told them everything they asked, like I'm telling you now. They too asked me for your number, and I couldn't, to save my life, remember it."

"You told them 'everything?'"

"Almost."

Xavier looked at Darleen, who in turn looked at something beyond his right ear. This bothered him. He turned to find out what it was exactly she kept looking at, but there was nothing to look at behind him.

"What didn't you tell them?"

"Darn," she said, "one of the cops asked me to make a list of all the things I had in my purse. Anyway, I told him everythin' except for my tampons." Darleen blushed when she said tampons.

"That's no big deal," Xavier said.

"My periods are bad," said Darleen. "My whole purse was full of them."

Xavier looked at her, then asked, "Did these guys have any visible scars, anything you remember? Were they tall, short, fat, skinny? Did one of them limp? Was the other missing an arm? What? What, for Christ-sakes?"

Darleen looked at the wall again.

"What is it?" asked Xavier. "What do you keep looking at?"

"Nothing. I just can't stand here facing you. I'm so sorry."

"Try to remember."

"I can't think under pressure like this. I stop up."

"What color were their eyes?" Xavier grew excited.

"I told the police what I remembered."

"Which isn't much, Darleen." He paused here to breathe. Oxygen wasn't penetrating his lungs.

"I'm sorry," was all Darleen said.

"And all this happened at..."

"Five after nine this morning."

Shit, Xavier thought, and sighed, *those bastards are long gone.* "Long gone," he said.

"Beg your pardon?"

"Nothing," he said.

"What happens now?" she asked.

It was one thing to be careless, but then not to remember anything. "Who knows," he said.

"You have every right to be upset with me," she said. "You can fire me."

"I'm not upset with you. It could've happened to anybody. And no, I'm not going to fire you."

Xavier stood and decided to brew some coffee.

"Would you like some coffee?" he asked.

"I'm too jittery and wound up—coffee's the last thing I need."

It was certainly the last thing *he* needed. There was something rising in him, and it wasn't anger or violence or any other emotion that was easily describable. His chest tightened and the tighter it felt, the louder his heartbeats sounded. His heart was at his throat. His ears burned.

Darleen noticed that there was something wrong. Her boss stood there in the corner of the room. "Here, let me fix it," she said, and came around to his side of the desk.

Xavier didn't move. Couldn't. Something sank in him, took a grip of his legs and arms and left him immobilized.

Darleen grabbed him by the arms and led him back to his desk chair. He sat down and stared at the wall in front of him. A poster of the Miami Dolphins' Dan Marino, number 13, hung there. The poster and several rows of Agent-of-the-Month awards from Prudential were the only decorations on the wall, but Xavier looked at them with a blank, pale look on his face.

"...So sorry, Mr. Cuevas," she was saying. "I really am, but what happened this morning wasn't my fault." She paused for approval.

"From now on I'll be more careful," she continued. "I'll enroll in a class. One of those self-defense crash courses. You know what I'm talking about? Learn to kick, grab and pull, that sort of thing."

But her boss was somewhere else where nothing he heard or saw or felt or smelled or tasted made any difference. Nothing fazed him. It was as if he'd been placed in one of those dark, sensory deprivation tanks.

Darleen tried to hide her nervousness behind a fixed smile as she put the filter with the coffee on the machine. She flipped on the switch and waited for the water to begin spurting out of the nozzle. She didn't know what to do about her boss, perhaps she should call someone. 9-1-1. An ambulance. The fire department's rescue unit. Xavier's wife might know what to do.

"You want me to call your wife?" she asked him.

He didn't respond.

Then the door opened and in walked Wilfredo. Darleen felt a wave of relief wash over her. She'd never been happier to see Wilfredo.

Wilfredo with his Miami Vice rerun look filtered through the Cuban psyche, for he—though he wanted to keep up with the latest trends in fashion and look hip—was a YUCA. Upwardly mobile, propelled by steady hits of Cuban coffee bought at To-Go windows of restaurants and cafeterias. Wilfredo walked in holding a styrofoam cup, a *colada*, of freshly brewed Cuban espresso. His eyes, normally wide and alert, were still bloodshot and puffy from a rough night.

"I'm so glad you're here," Darleen said as she met him by his office.

"Good morning to you, too, Blanca Nieves," he said and smiled. This was what he called her, which meant Snow White.

Darleen followed Wilfredo to his desk, where he put down the cup and then slipped out of his jacket. "Want a hit?" he said as he uncapped the cup and poured himself a shot.

"Something's wrong," she said.

"Ah, nothing better to perk you up." He looked at the note Xavier had left him on his desk. "The boss man here?"

"He is..."

"What's the matter, Darleen? You look a little nervous." Wilfredo pronounced her name weird, making it almost sound like *Darling*.

"A little, hell..."

He drank another shot of the espresso and stood up.

"So the boss man's in, eh?" he asked.

"Yes," she told him, "he's in there. There's something not right with him."

"Not right?"

Wilfredo walked into his partner's office. Xavier was sitting in the chair. Wilfredo looked at Darleen as if she were playing a joke on him.

"He's comatose," she said.

"Comawhat?" Wilfredo said, then to Xavier, "I think Darleen's losing it, bro."

Xavier wasn't saying anything. His face was pale, almost translucent, sweat had broken out all over his face, matting strands of his hair to his wet forehead. He shivered as if the temperature in the room had dipped below freezing.

"Quick, Darleen," said Wilfredo, "call 9-1-1."

Xavier raised a hand to stop them from doing so.

"What's going on, X?" Wilfredo asked.

"Don't call anybody," Xavier spoke.

"What's up?"

"Freezing."

Wilfredo removed his coat and put it on his partner's back. Wilfredo was confused; he didn't know what the situation was. Wilfredo looked into his partner's blank staring eyes and said, "Hey, buddy, what's the matter?"

"It's freezing in here," he said.

"Let me call an ambulance," Darleen said.

"No, no ambulance, I said. Don't call anybody," Xavier spoke slowly.

Wilfredo grabbed Xavier's cold hands and held them long enough to warm them up a little. Xavier's hands were limp, lifeless.

"Get me some paper towels," Wilfredo said to Darleen. She hurried away, then came back with a wad of Kleenex. She gave them to Wilfredo, who placed them on his partner's sweaty forehead. Wiping along with one hand, Wilfredo felt Xavier's pulse with the other. The pulse quickened; the breathing became highly irregular. Xavier gasped for air.

Xavier, he realized, was suffering from some kind of anxiety or panic attack. "Hold on, X," he said to his partner, then to Darleen, "Come out here a minute."

She followed him outside to her desk. "What happened?" Wilfredo asked Darleen.

She told him about getting mugged and about the stolen money. She said: "He said it was Segovia's money."

"Whose money?"

"An important client." Darleen leaned against the door frame. She had a scared expression on her face.

"I think we should call 9-1-1," she said.

"No calls," Xavier said from his office.

Wilfredo returned to his partner's office.

"What do you want us to do?" Wilfredo said.

"Get me out of here," Xavier said. "I've got to get out of here."

Wilfredo helped Xavier get up off the chair. "Okay," Wilfredo told him, "where do you wanna go?"

"Take him to the doctor," Darleen said.

"No doctors," Xavier told her.

"No doctors," Wilfredo said. "Okay."

"To the beach. To my father's."

"One minute he was talking to me..." she said. "He looked okay. Then he stood up and didn't say anything. Just stood there like a store-window dummy."

"To the beach it is," replied Wilfredo.

They walked out slowly.

"We're going in my car," Wilfredo said to Darleen.

"Should we call his wife?"

"I'll call her," Wilfredo said.

Darleen and Wilfredo took Xavier into the elevator—thank God it was empty, Wilfredo thought—and downstairs to the parking lot. As they tried to sit Xavier in Wilfredo's Camaro, Xavier's head bumped against the door frame several times before they managed to sit him down and strap him in.

"What a shitty day," Darleen said.

Wilfredo found the beeper hooked to his partner's belt and removed it. Then he turned to Darleen. "Please, dig up...what's his name again?"

"Who?"

"The man, the money."

"Segovia."

"Leave his file on my desk."

He showed the beeper to Darleen and said, "Beep me if something important comes up."

"You'll be at the beach, right?" she asked.

"Fresh air," Xavier said.

"The beach, right. Plenty of fresh air there."

Wilfredo climbed into the driver's seat, started the engine—it grumbled and flared up—and drove out of the parking lot in a hurry. Behind the car, by the entrance, Darleen stood bracing herself.

On the busy streets, Wilfredo weaved in and out between the cars. He was speeding, for the faster he got to the Art Deco district in Miami Beach where Carlos Antonio lived, the better his partner would feel, even though Wilfredo didn't know how Xavier's father would help.

The Camaro sped eastward on the expressway. At the toll by the Orange Bowl, Wilfredo rolled down the window and threw a quarter into the basket. Then, once the red- and white-striped bar rose, he stepped on the gas. They rode over the Miami River away from the downtown buildings. The Centrust stuck out of the ground like someone's middle finger. What a monstrosity. Past the *Miami Herald's* baby-shit-colored office building, he drove over a drawbridge and saw how the loud humdrum of the wheels going over the bridge's metal grid startled Xavier.

Once on the McArthur Causeway, Wilfredo watched how the needle of the speedometer quivered at 85 miles per hour. The car zoomed past the charter fishing boat docks, helicopter rides, Chalks Airline platforms, and trash-cluttered foliage. Flocks of sea birds swarmed over the docked cruise ships.

With a fixed stare, Xavier looked at the water. A brown pelican glided as fast as the car moved.

Incredible, those bastards can really fly!

Welcome to Miami Beach. Wilfredo brought his partner here. Nothing like fresh air and also the panoramic view of the ocean to bring Xavier back, Wilfredo thought.

They found themselves driving along Collins Avenue, then Ocean Drive, the main artery in the heart of the Art Deco District.

"Here we are," Wilfredo said. Xavier was sitting still, staring blankly at all the scenery.

Most of the buildings, having been built during the thirties, were painted in bright pastels. Soft colors: lilac, pink, yellow, azure, baby blue. The landmarks stood now as a hip/cool, tropical setting, erect in all their glamour by 23rd Street, Ocean Drive, 5th Street, and Lenox Court. The hotel and building names here sounded exotic and tropical: Tropics, I Paparazzi, Adrian, Revere Hotel, Café de Artes, Beacon, The Palace Bar, Leslie, The Carlysle, Crescent Hotel, Netherland, Winter Haven, and the Cardoso Hotel, which was presently being restored.

It was where Carlos Antonio lived.

Blackbirds sat atop the telephone wires preening their feathers. They looked like tar droplets sagging on the line, strung up like beads.

Parking was a hassle, but Wilfredo and Xavier got lucky. Right in front of the Cardoso Hotel, somebody pulled out of a metered space. Wilfredo, after signaling, quickly maneuvered, parked, and got out of the car. He came around the front and opened the door for Xavier.

"Sunshine City," he said as he helped Xavier climb out of the car. Then, "Feeling better?"

Xavier stood there and didn't reply.

"Look at that ocean," Wilfredo continued. "Smell that air. Nothing cleaner than that."

In the distance people played volleyball on the sand.

The expression on Xavier's face remained one of detachment. His startled eyes focused on nothing in particular.

A pleasant, slight breeze ruffled the tops of the palm trees.

"C'mon, buddy," Wilfredo said, "you'll be all right. Wait and see."

Wilfredo got Xavier's wallet out of the back pocket of his pants. As Wilfredo looked through the wallet, an old lady, her purse safely tucked under her arms, shuffled by and mumbled something about all the perverts at the beach.

"Got your father's card?" Wilfredo said to Xavier. "Right? We need the apartment number. You know the number, X?"

Xavier didn't answer.

Carlos Antonio resided at the Cardoso, that much Xavier had mentioned to him before, but he didn't know on what floor or in what apartment.

In the wallet were pictures of Sarah, Sarah and the children, Eric (who was Wilfredo's godchild) and Lindy, Eric alone dressed in a peewee league baseball uniform, and of Lindy hugging a pillow and sucking her thumb. The business cards were mixed in with credit cards. Wilfredo removed all the cards from the folds of the wallet and fingered through them one by one.

"Bingo!" Wilfredo said, finding Carlos Antonio's business card.

Wilfredo put all the cards back into the wallet and returned it to Xavier's pocket. He led his partner across the street to the entrance of the hotel.

They entered the cool lobby of the hotel and headed straight for the elevator. Once inside the elevator, Wilfredo pressed the second-floor button and the door took a long time to close.

"Fucking slow door," Wilfredo said.

As the elevator rode up slowly, its overhead air vent hummed and made a faint clicking sound. The door opened and they walked out of the elevator into the hallway. An apartment-number directory arrow pointed Wilfredo in the right direction. Forty-five was the last apartment on the east side of the building.

They halted at the door. Wilfredo knocked. No reply. He knocked again, and again no answer.

Inside the apartment the knocking surprised a man who napped on the sofa by the opened window. When he heard the knocking, the man sprang up and contemplated what to do. He decided to approach the door and peek to see who it was.

Wilfredo tried once more, this time as loud as possible.

The man saw two men. The dark one he didn't recognize, but the other one with the listless expression looked familiar. The man thought he remembered Xavier from someplace. Then, instead of answering the door, he tiptoed to the bedroom and examined a framed snapshot of a young man and his family. The face in the picture was the same as the one he saw through the peephole, but who was the other man?

"No one's home," Wilfredo said to Xavier.

Wilfredo took his pen and an old credit-card receipt and began to write Carlos Antonio a note when the door opened.

The man behind the door put his foot in the way so as not to let the two men have a better look inside. They had to speak to one another through the narrow opening.

"Is Carlos Antonio here?" Wilfredo asked.

"*El Salió*," the man said in Spanish, meaning that Carlos Antonio had gone out.

There was a moment of awkward silence as both Wilfredo and the man looked at Xavier's "gone" expression. Wilfredo spoke to him in Spanish, *"Es el hijo de Carlos Antonio."*

The man opened the door and let Xavier and Wilfredo inside the apartment.

"Who are you?" the man asked.

"We work together," Wilfredo answered. "I'm Wilfredo, his office partner."

"Adolfo," the man introduced himself.

The place was decorated with wicker and bamboo furniture, baskets, and brightly colored cushions. After Adolfo closed and locked the door, he joined Xavier and Wilfredo in the living room.

"I didn't mean to be rude," he said, "but I thought you were somebody else."

There was a magnificent view of the beach and the ocean from where they stood. The heads of the scattered swimmers looked like buoys in the distance.

"Please, have a seat," Adolfo said.

Going Under

Adolfo sat down on the sofa and tucked his veiny, bare feet under him. He was dressed in jeans and a Miami Hurricanes T-shirt. Adolfo was thin and tall, with longish arms and legs, and an Adam's apple which made him look goofy. Ruddy was his complexion. Adolfo's deep-set, hollowed eyes were brown, intense.

Wilfredo sat Xavier across from Adolfo on a wicker easy chair with flower-print cushions. Xavier stared straight at the view.

"What's wrong with him?" Adolfo asked.

"He's had a rough day," Wilfredo said.

"It's not even noon yet."

"You're looking at a hard-core workaholic."

"Why didn't you take him to a doctor?" Adolfo asked.

"He wanted to come here," Wilfredo said.

"Carlos Antonio'll be back soon," Adolfo said, and then lit a cigarette. He leaned back on the wicker sofa and exhaled, plumes of smoke floating in front of his unshaven face. His cheekbones and jaw protruded under the thin taut skin on his face. The nose, too, was thin but far from straight. It seemed Adolfo's nose had been broken several times and poorly reset each time.

The wicker creaked at the slightest movement.

Wilfredo, now that he was sitting down, noticed his nervousness. "Do you mind?" he said, and pointed at Adolfo's cigarettes.

"Help yourself," Adolfo said, and reached over to hand them to Wilfredo.

Wilfredo took a cigarette from the pack and lit it. They smoked in silence for a while. Both tried not to stare at Xavier, who continued to look out the window.

"I wonder how long this'll last?" Wilfredo said.

"Depends on the person," said Adolfo. "How much time they rest. When I was in Angola, I saw a lot of soldiers like this, and it lasted a couple of days. Sometimes longer."

"You fought in Angola?"

"Two tours of duty. In the late seventies."

Seemed like such a long time ago, Wilfredo thought, he and Xavier were almost seniors in high school. Wilfredo looked at Xavier, who sat up rigidly, his fingers clutched around the chair's armrest.

Adolfo said, "Carlos Antonio should return soon. If he doesn't, I'll call him at the office."

The cigarette smoke made Wilfredo cough.

"Something to drink?" Adolfo asked.

"A beer saves the day."

Adolfo went into the kitchen, opened the refrigerator, grabbed a couple of bottles, and brought them back. The bottles started to sweat and circles of water formed on the glass of the bamboo coffee table on which sat a bronze, horse-head cane, a clay candelabra with red candles, and a carved gourd.

"Better call Carlos Antonio," Adolfo said. After a long pull of beer, he got up and went over to use the kitchen phone. He dialed Carlos Antonio's office number.

Adolfo hung up. "Carlos Antonio is on his way," he said.

Adolfo walked over and stood by Xavier. Looking Xavier over, he said, "What your friend here needs is lots of rest and relaxation. Maybe we should put him in bed."

Wilfredo helped Adolfo take his partner to the bedroom. Carlos Antonio's bedroom was clean and orga-
nized, with little furniture. The queen-size sleigh bed
was to one side of the room under the Levelor blinds of
the window. By the head of the bed rested a large porce-
lain vase with ceiling-high black bamboo sticks.

Once Xavier was in bed, Adolfo removed his shoes
and put a blanket over him. He then closed the blinds so
the bright sunlight wouldn't bother Xavier.

"Hey, X," Wilfredo said to his partner, "I'm gonna go,
all right? Don't worry, I'll take care of everything."

"Try to rest," said Adolfo.

Xavier closed his eyes.

"Your father'll be here soon," Wilfredo said, and
backed away from the bed. Then, looking at Adolfo, he
said, "I'll leave you the office number. If anything happens, tell Carlos Antonio to call me, please."

"I will."

Adolfo led Wilfredo to the door and said, "I know
someone who can help your friend."

"Good," Wilfredo said, and stepped out into the hallway. "He needs all the help he can get."

Adolfo closed the door and locked it immediately
after they said goodbye. Wilfredo tracked his way down
the hallway and back to the elevator.

Back to the things he had to do. Talk to someone at
Prudential's main office about Segovia's money. That
money had to be replaced. It was then that Wilfredo
began to realize how complicated his partner's life was—
too many strings pulling him apart.

Carlos Antonio asked a doctor friend to come over and take a look at Xavier. The physician, a man in his early fifties, bald, wire-rimmed glasses in front of large peeled eyes, thoroughly examined Xavier. "Stress," the doctor said. "He's got his heartbeat going fast. Faster than the space shuttle in orbit. High blood pressure, too. Overwork and anxiety. He'll be fine, let him rest."

After the doctor left, Carlos Antonio returned to the living room and joined Adolfo on the sofa, where they both watched the news on television. During a commercial, Adolfo told Carlos Antonio about the person he knew who could help Xavier.

The phone rang. Adolfo walked over and answered. Wilfredo's voice came on the line. He was calling from the office, wanted to know how Xavier was doing. Adolfo waved Carlos Antonio over and handed him the phone.

"*¿Qué pasa?*" Carlos Antonio said.

"How is he?" Wilfredo asked.

Carlos Antonio repeated what his doctor friend had concluded about his son's situation.

"Overworked is right," Wilfredo said. "He was working too much, you know. Didn't have a moment of rest. I think the trouble with Segovia, one of his clients, did him in."

"What trouble?" Carlos Antonio asked.

Wilfredo explained the situation with Segovia's policy money. After thinking it over, Carlos Antonio agreed to lend Xavier the money until they found a way to recoup the losses.

"Should I go by and see Sarah?" Wilfredo asked Carlos Antonio.

"Will you do that, please?" said Carlos Antonio. "I'll call her myself, but please go by and see her and the children. Tell her what has happened. That everything's under control."

"I'll call you tomorrow," Wilfredo said, and hung up.

If he called Sarah, Carlos Antonio wondered, what would she think? He didn't want to alarm her. So, Carlos Antonio's best bet was to get a hold of Mirna and have her call Sarah.

"Would you like a sandwich?" Carlos Antonio asked.

"Not hungry, thanks," said Adolfo, who leaned all the way back on the sofa and made himself comfortable by putting a couple of cushions under his head.

He dialed his ex-wife's number. Mirna answered and was quickly taken aback by the sound of Carlos' voice. He told her what had happened.

"I saw him yesterday," she said. "He was fine."

"Don't worry," he told her, "he's fine now."

"Are you taking him to a hospital?"

To calm her down, he said, "The doctor already saw him."

"Why did he go to you?" she asked in an indignant tone of voice.

"Wilfredo brought him here," he admitted. "It was *his* idea." Then he told her what he wanted her to do, which was to call Sarah and tell her not to worry, that Xavier was in good hands.

When he said "in good hands" Mirna chuckled, and to disguise it she assured Carlos Antonio that, yes, she'd give their daughter-in-law a call.

"Tell her Xavier'll be staying here for a couple of days," said Carlos Antonio.

Mirna, though she didn't agree, consented to do her ex-husband the favor.

Carlos Antonio said goodbye and hung up. Once he was through making the sandwiches, he returned to the sofa and joined Adolfo, who now watched a game show.

It seemed like it was always the same show host, same participants, same audience...but today had been such a draining day that Carlos Antonio surrendered to its simplicity and let it entertain him.

But soon enough the phone rang. This time he answered. It was Sarah, wanting to know what Xavier was doing there. Why couldn't he come home? To his family? She was upset, all right.

"Sarita, relax," he told her. "He's okay."

"I'm going over right now," she said.

Sarah arrived, sat in the bedroom, and watched Xavier sleep. That was all he did: sleep. She didn't understand what was happening. She sat on the edge of the bed and looked at her husband sleep. He didn't stir awake. This was the man, she thought, for whom she had given up a singing career. She remembered the time they went up to Illinois to visit her parents. Little did they know that she had gotten pregnant during that visit. Her parents were wishy-washy about Xavier. Getting pregnant upset her because she realized during her last months in Tucson that she'd never sing professionally. Indeed, she wondered if having failed at making their—hers and Xavier's—dreams come true had brought them closer together. They believed they loved each other, so toward the end of their stay in Tucson, they decided to keep the baby and move to Miami to begin a new life.

She sat still for a long time, feeling lost and saddened. As the afternoon drew to an end, she decided to leave. She figured Carlos Antonio was right, no sense in trying to disturb him. Xavier was out. If he returned home with her, the children would drill him with questions. The children, she understood, shouldn't see their daddy like this.

Outside in the living room, she found the skinny man and her father-in-law playing checkers. Neither one seemed to notice her.

"I'm going home," she said.

"Oh, Sarita," Carlos Antonio said, "please stay. Have dinner with us."

"I have to get back to the children," she told him. "I left them with a friend. Thank you." She had never told Carlos Antonio this, but she didn't like it whenever he called her Sarita.

"Some other time then," he said.

"Sure."

Carlos Antonio got up to walk Sarah to the door. He always felt awkward around Sarah, he thought, and he couldn't pin down the reason. Maybe it was that he felt

Sarah was a little snobbish. She wasn't pretty; she was beautiful, and in his mind he always thought of her as *La Americana*.

"Don't walk me down," she said in a harsher tone than she intended. "I parked far away. I'll walk."

"Fine," he said, and opened the door for her. "Give the children a big kiss for me."

"Tell him to call me as soon as he..." she said, and stopped.

"Don't worry, I will."

Sarah left. As soon as she was gone, Carlos Antonio made up his mind to get to the bottom of Xavier's problems and place him back on track.

Xavier did nothing but sleep and rest. No sleeplessness to stir up any old ghosts for him. He slept through Wilfredo's visit when Wilfredo came to pick up the money Carlos Antonio had offered in order to replace Segovia's stolen cash. Even when Sarah and Mirna visited, Xavier continued to sleep. It was as though he'd been given a sleep potion from which he'd never awake.

After three days, he finally woke up. The first thing he did was complain about how hungry he was. This was a good sign according to Carlos Antonio, who brought his son food from all the area restaurants. Xavier ate with renewed appetite, a voracity only equalled when he played soccer. He didn't feel like talking or thinking much, but to get up and move about brought him energy.

In the afternoon of the third day, Xavier shaved, showered, and put on a clean shirt and the most comfortable pair of slacks Sarah had left for him. Standing in front of the bedroom window, Xavier looked out at the sea. The water sparkled in the distance. A cruise ship cut the water as it headed south, leaving a ribbon of smoke lingering in the air. As it headed for the horizon, it grew smaller and smaller.

The dark smoke dissipated in the air.

"How are you feeling?" Carlos Antonio asked him.

"Umm," he uttered.

"Don't feel like talking, eh?"

He shook his head.

Though he felt calmer and more relaxed, there was still something missing. Deep roots of confusion and angst had taken hold of Xavier's mind and soul. At best, Xavier felt lost. Something told him that he didn't belong. He didn't know the source of his detachment. He felt that the voice he heard coming from outside the room didn't belong to his father, someone he'd always known and cared about, but was a stranger's. Sure, he felt a little paranoid, too.

When he heard his father and Adolfo speaking in Spanish, the language of Xavier's infancy, vague memories bombarded Xavier. Memories of a simpler, happier time, when he was a child, when his parents lived in the same house, when his roots were still connected to and nurtured by parental love and care.

With the help of Adolfo, Carlos Antonio made an appointment to see a woman called Caledonia. A *santera*.

"When you get there," Adolfo said, "tell her I sent you. She'll move you up in the line."

"Line?" Carlos Antonio said.

"She's very busy," said Adolfo, "but she *will* see you when she hears I sent you."

According to Adolfo, Caledonia specialized in help-ing people in distress. People who claimed to have lost their way. Caledonia was the woman who had let Adolfo stay in her garage when he had first gotten to Miami from Mariel.

Carlos Antonio and Xavier drove out of Miami Beach and went to see Caledonia. Outside, all the traffic made the streets seem strange, foreign to Xavier, who didn't recognize where he was. On the way very little was said between Carlos Antonio and his son.

When his father asked him how he felt, Xavier didn't say anything, and when he did answer, it was in English, in the language that was most familiar to him, but one he all of a sudden failed to understand. All he knew was that the words formed all by themselves in the back of his brain and came forth and out of his mouth unwilled.

"Are you depressed?" Carlos Antonio wanted to know.

Xavier thought about depression. He'd really never suffered from mood swings. But discussing his mental health made him all the more uncomfortable. *Depres-*

sion. It was a strange word. He contemplated ways to help himself without really having to go to a psychologist or psychiatrist the way his mother and Sarah recommended. All he knew about psychoanalysts was that they always suggested talking about your feelings and emotions. All that let's-talk-about-your-childhood, tell-me-about-your-mother stuff. The last thing Xavier wanted to do was think about his past when he no longer felt he had one.

Caledonia owned a *botánica* shop on Calle Ocho in the heart of Little Havana on the outskirts of downtown Miami. From the outside, the shop looked small and crowded, tucked between two larger buildings, one a furniture retail store and the other a hardware store. A flashing neon sign read CALEDONIA'S.

Carlos Antonio parked the car in front of the place. Father and son got out and approached the wrought-iron screen door at the entrance. Located by the doorbell was a hand, fingers together, painted in white and outlined in black.

Carlos Antonio pressed the button twice, waited, then a short woman appeared behind the screen. Her big and black eyes stood out on her small, sad-looking face.

"¿Tienen cita?" She asked in Spanish whether they had an appointment. Her voice sounded tired and rough as though she'd been up the whole night talking. She spoke with a Nicaraguan accent.

"Adolfo sent us," Carlos Antonio said.

She unlocked the door and let them in. A thick scent of jasmine incense greeted them in the lobby. The place was full of shelves and on the shelves stood all kinds of Saint and Virgin statuettes. Also black dolls, African deities, real fruit on plates, jars and glasses full of pennies. Beads hung in looping W's from the shelves. By the corner stood a life-size statue of San Lázaro holding on to his crutches, letting two life-size dogs lick his bleeding leprous sores.

Inside a glass counter sat miniatures of more Saints and Virgins, dried mango and mamey seeds. Powders. Cigars. Shiny vermillion-colored pebbles. Feather amulets. Charmed ribbons and scrolls. On top of the counter rested an old, cast-iron cash register, the kind with the pop-up numbers.

"I'm Fabiola," the woman said. "Caledonia's aide."

Carlos Antonio introduced Xavier first, then himself, and was about to ask how long of a wait they had when a deep, resonant, scratchy voice came from the back room.

"Señor Cuevas?" the voice said.

"That's me," Carlos Antonio answered.

"Adolfo called me to tell me you were coming," Caledonia said from an unseen place. Then to the woman, "Fabiola, take the gentlemen to consultation room two."

"*Sí, mi santa, como no,*" said Fabiola.

On the way down a long hall, they passed a waiting room in which the people there were sitting quietly, reading through magazines and newspapers. Fabiola led them to a small room. There was nothing but a wicker chair and several pillows strewn on the floor. On the wall in front of them stood a row of lit candles. Sunlight snuck in through the parted, heavy curtains. Moats of dust danced in the rays of light.

"Sit down," Fabiola said. "*La Santísima* will be with you shortly." Then she closed the door behind her and left Carlos Antonio and Xavier alone in the room. Xavier's hands sweated as he kept asking himself *What am I doing here?* He looked at his father, but Carlos Antonio only smiled.

They waited for what felt like a long time. Just when Xavier was about to sit down on the wicker chair, the door opened and a fat woman dressed in a white tunic and a white scarf for a turban entered the room. She was smoking a cigar stub whose pungent odor reached Xavier's nostrils as quickly as she entered.

Necklaces of red and black beads covered Caledonia's neck. She extended her fat hand for father and son to shake, or was it for them to kiss? She had a pleasant look on her face. Baby talcum powder residue clung to her cheeks and chin as if she'd just come out of the shower. Her eyes, during that first moment while Xavier shook her hand and gazed into them, seemed to sparkle.

"Xavier." She said his name correctly, then let go of his hand. "Have a seat."

"Did Adolfo tell you why we've come to see you?" Carlos Antonio asked, and sat down on one of the floor pillows.

"He told me about the..." She looked at Xavier, then said, "...the situation." She sat down on the wicker chair, which made cracking and popping sounds under her weight. Looking directly at Xavier, she said, "I believe I can help you." Then she turned to Carlos Antonio and said, "Will you be kind enough to leave us alone, please?"

He stood up and left the room. Caledonia smiled and looked into Xavier's troubled eyes. "Tell me about yourself," she said.

"What do you want to know?"

"*Todo*, everything."

Reluctant at first, Xavier spoke slowly, filling gaps of conversation with silence, then not so self-conscious anymore, he told Caledonia everything he could about his aspirations of one day making a lot of money in the insurance business, but yet all that had been undermined by a strong feeling of detachment and dislocation. Insecurities plagued him, so he no longer knew what he wanted to do, or whether what he was doing meant anything. Things, as they happened fast, were falling apart.

"Are you Cuban or American?" she asked.

"I feel more American than I do Cuban."

"But you're not Cuban. That is, you don't *feel* Cuban."

Xavier nodded.

She studied the young man for a while as if in a trance, then stood up and called Fabiola. Fabiola opened the door and stuck her head in.

"*Prepara las cosas para una limpieza y llamada*," Caledonia said, instructing Fabiola to prepare things for a cleansing and a summons.

Then to Xavier she said, "Take off your clothes and lie on the floor with your limbs spread out."

Thinking about Caledonia being nothing but a quack and a fake who was only after cheap thrills, Xavier hesitated, but out of indifference did what she told him. While he stripped, she walked around him and poked her finger into places on his back, shoulder blades, stomach, rib cage, thighs, and buttocks. "Looking for," she said, "the ideal place for the entrance." She stopped to chew the cigar.

On his belly button, she placed her fist and hit twice, then she brought her fist up to her face, closed her eyes and tilted her head back. "The Orishas will help you."

Fabiola returned with a tray and placed it on the floor next to the wicker chair. On the tray was a mother-of-pearl-handled razor blade, a set of red and black pill boxes with powders in them. Once again Fabiola left the room only to return a moment later with a live white dove in her hands.

Xavier stretched out on the floor. Caledonia, barefooted, kept circling above him. On one of her ankles was a tattoo, a symbol of some kind, and on the other was an anklet made out of red, white, and black tamarind seeds. She stopped to light her cigar stub, which she turned and turned in her mouth as she chewed.

The smoke from the cigar hung in front of her face like a silken kerchief. It brought her face a distant look of anguish. Fabiola approached Caledonia. In her hands the dove looked scared. Its head twitched nervously.

In a trance, Caledonia chanted in an Afro-Cuban dialect. All Xavier understood were the names, Changó,

Elleggua, Ochun, Yemayá—names of African deities. *Las Siete Potencias.* The Orishas.

"Elleggua, Divine Trickster Linguist," Caledonia said, "Chief Engineer of the *Da* force and Lord of the *Nommo!*" Then she shouted out something in an Afro-Cuban dialect.

From the tray Caledonia lifted the razor blade, opened it. With one hand she held the razor and with the other the dove. She held it by its legs. The dove fluttered about. Then with a swift movement she sliced the dove's head off. The head landed between Xavier's legs. Caledonia held the body over him and sprinkled the blood on his chest and stomach.

She moved so quickly now that Xavier believed she was floating about the room. She screamed, groaned and moaned, and then she swooped down on Xavier and smeared more blood on his face. Her cold hands rubbed his arms, legs, and loins.

Softly, she said, "Elleggua, go away! Take with you all that which is chaotic, absurd, unpredictable, and impossible. Go away, mischievous child! Go away, ancient wise man! Take your trickery with you. Elleggua warrior. *¡LÁRGATE!*"

Caledonia knew that, when pleased, Elleggua could not only save the life of a person in danger but also bestow unexpected good fortune and destiny. When angered, Elleggua could cause untold havoc and despair in a person's life.

Elleggua's altar was kept on the floor behind the front door. It was there Fabiola went and lit the seven candles.

By now Xavier couldn't keep his eyes open. It was then he got the shivers. Convulsions came and went, and he lost all sense of time and space. He faded, still resisting belief in the messy ritual.

When Xavier awoke, he was clean and a towel covered his naked midsection. He was still on the floor, a pillow under his head. Caledonia and Fabiola were gone.

Feeling a little shaky and dizzy, Xavier stood up and got dressed. Just when he was about finished dressing, Carlos Antonio walked in.

"How do you feel?" Carlos Antonio asked.

Xavier told him he didn't feel any different. As they both walked out of the room and retraced their steps back to the lobby and front room, he asked, "How long was I in there?"

Carlos Antonio said, "Two or three hours. I stepped out to have lunch."

Fabiola stood behind the counter and cash register in the front room. She acted as though nothing had happened. Xavier told her he wanted to see Caledonia.

"Oh, Señor Cuevas," she said. "*La Santísima* is resting. She's asleep now. She told me to tell you that the spirit is with you."

"Spirit?"

"The spirit the Orishas chose to guide you."

Fabiola wrote down on a receipt the amount for the consultation. Carlos Antonio paid her and, as they walked out of the place into a cloudy afternoon, he thought that maybe all of this had been nothing but a foolish mistake.

Xavier, of course, was thinking about the spirit. *The spirit the Orishas chose to guide you.* The words lingered in Xavier's head as Carlos Antonio drove his son home.

Listening to the news on the radio in Carlos Antonio's new Mercedes, Xavier felt a strange sensation. A light-headedness. To avoid the discomfort, Xavier concentrated on the news. Sports. Jimmy Johnson and the University of Miami Hurricanes had won yet another important game, this one against Notre Dame's Fighting Irish.

Driving up to the house, Xavier saw Sarah's car in the driveway. Eric rode his skateboard up and down the sidewalk. At first Xavier didn't recognize his own son. The boy's blond hair was wet and combed back. He wore an Ocean Pacific T-shirt and knee-length shorts torn and dirtied at the pockets. Eric, who rigged up a ramp with a couple of bricks and a flat board, skated as fast as he could and jumped.

Xavier's father rolled down the window and shouted, "*¡Rubio!*"

Eric swerved and stopped in time not to hit his grandfather's car as it turned into the driveway.

"Don't call me that, Grandpa!" Eric said. *Rubio* meant blondie.

"Don't call me Grandpa," Carlos Antonio said, getting out of the car and hugging and kissing the boy. "It makes me old. But if you must, call me *Abuelo*."

Eric was either puzzled or he was squinting at the sun, for he asked, "What's the difference?" He understood Spanish but refused to speak it.

Xavier climbed out of the car, realizing that three days weren't long enough of an absence for Eric to miss him. Besides, Sarah probably had told the children he'd gone on a business trip. The boy carried on with his grandfather about Carlos Antonio's new car.

"You want to go for a drive?" Carlos Antonio asked him.

"Really?" said Eric.

"Ask your mother first."

Speaking of Sarah, she was standing at the door looking directly at the two men and her son. There were times when she asked herself how she ever got involved with this culture, and this was one of those times. Xavier noticed Sarah leaning against the door frame.

"Go ahead," she said, "but don't take too long."

"We'll be right back," Carlos Antonio told his daughter-in-law. Then to Eric he said, "Climb in, *Rubio*."

"Don't call me that!" said Eric as he climbed into the car on the driver's side and moved over to the passenger seat.

Carlos Antonio got in, too, started the car and drove away.

Xavier felt awkward being back.

"How are you feeling?" she asked.

"Okay, I guess," Xavier said.

Sarah hugged him. He held her tight, his hands caressing the small of her back. "I worried about you," she said. "What happened?"

"I don't know."

She let go and walked inside, waited for her husband to enter, and then closed the door.

"Where's Lindy?"

"She's over at Carmen's house." Carmen was Lindy's school friend. "She's been sleeping there. Since you weren't here..."

After a long awkward pause, Sarah again asked what happened. Xavier tried to explain, but something blocked his memory. He honestly didn't remember much, except being at the office, then finding himself at his father's apartment with Adolfo.

He told her about Adolfo, which led him into talking about Caledonia. What Xavier didn't tell Sarah was that Caledonia had performed a cleansing. *Una limpieza.* Being even less superstitious than he, Sarah wouldn't understand. The idea of someone doing *brujería* baffled her. When the controversy about the *santería* church in Hialeah, where animals were being sacrificed, broke out on the local news, Sarah voiced her concern about how cruelty to animals should not be allowed.

What would she think of the summons? Xavier held Sarah's hand. Her long and straight fingers ended in perfectly manicured nails. The moons of her fingernails stood out against the shellacked mauve polish. "Do you remember the time the burglars broke into the house in Tucson?" he asked.

Sarah thought back and remembered. Late one night, while they slept, a couple of high school punks broke in, thinking no one was home. They shattered the kitchen door and walked in. The noise startled Xavier awake, then he heard the young voices. Hanging from the bedpost, he grabbed the gas mask one of his teammates had given him as a reminder of the team's inside joke about the coach passing gas during halftime. Xavier put the gas mask on and walked out of the bedroom. Sarah didn't know what the hell he was doing, but she went along because Xavier put his hand over her mouth. In the living room the boys worked quickly to disconnect the cables from the stereo. Xavier, sneaking up on the boys, switched on the light and at the same time screamed, "NOW SARAH! RELEASE THE GAS!" Needless to say that the boys' faces turned white when they saw Xavier. He was naked except for the gas mask. They dropped everything and ran out of the house. He was laughing when Sarah came out of the bedroom, then Xavier told her about the expression on the boys' faces.

"I've been thinking of all the fun we've had together," Xavier said.

"That *was* funny," she said.

"Just been thinking about it, that's all."

"What do you want to do?"

"Take it easy for a while," Xavier said.

"Do it," said Sarah. Then, "I've decided to take some time off myself. I've had a lot on my mind, too."

"Maybe we should go away."

"I am. I'm taking the children to Illinois."

Hearing that made Xavier's heartbeat quicken. "Just you and the children?" he asked.

"I need time to sort things out."

"Leave the children."

"My parents want to spend time with them."

Sarah stood up and approached the door because she thought she heard a car drive up. She opened the door, but Carlos Antonio and Eric were not back.

"Dad probably took Eric for some ice cream."

What Sarah said next took Xavier by surprise.

"Things are not going right," she said, turning around to face her husband. "I think we need time away from each other."

What should have taken but a few seconds to assimilate felt as though it would take years. Sarah's words were simple, direct, loud and clear, so why couldn't he understand what she was saying?

"What do you mean?" he asked.

"It's clear to me, Xavier," she said, "we have been growing apart for quite a long time."

"I realize I haven't been spending as much time as..."

"It isn't that."

By this point Xavier couldn't help but think about the worst scenario: *Sarah's having an affair. What did she want, a divorce?*

"We don't communicate anymore."

He got up and walked to the door. "I've missed you."

She said, "We take each other for granted these days."

"You feel I haven't been spending enough time with you and the children, and you're right. But that's all going to change."

"I need time to think."

Is she having an affair? Because if she is, I can't take it. Not in the shape I'm in.

She returned to the sofa and sat down. "We should separate for a while."

"I don't understand." *Separate, separate, separation...*

"All I'm asking for is a little time off, that's all. I'm thinking of going to New York, giving singing another try."

Carlos Antonio and Eric returned. Eric was excited by some of the things his grandfather had been telling him about the car's engine, like it being fuel-injected and computerized.

"Kiss your *abuelo* goodbye, Erico," Carlos Antonio called after the boy.

"Don't call me that."

Eric finally kissed his grandfather goodbye. Xavier thanked his father for the ride and the stay at the apartment. "Stay for dinner," Xavier said.

"I can't," he said.

"Give Sarah my love," Carlos Antonio said, got back in the Mercedes, and drove off.

Eric picked up his skateboard from the grass where he'd dropped it and took it to the back. Xavier heard Brandy barking.

"I want to see Lindy," he said to Sarah.

"Let's go pick her up."

And so they went to pick up their daughter, but since they took Eric with them they couldn't talk, and Xavier more than ever felt like he needed to talk to his wife. *Let things out.* Communicate, as Sarah put it.

Later when they got back to the house, Xavier picked up the phone and dialed Caledonia's number. Fabiola answered. He asked her to put Caledonia on, that it was an emergency. Fabiola put the phone on the counter by the register and went to Caledonia's room. After a long silence, Caledonia came on.

"Caledonia," he said. "This is Xavier."

"Yes, Xavier, what can I do for you?"

"I've been thinking about all this," he said, "and there's a slight problem."

"What is that?"

"I don't believe in spirits."

Caledonia laughed, and her laughter took on a weird quality. Not a shriek. It was a healthy, guttural laughter. She said, "Oh, but you do believe, you do believe in spirits."

After having dinner with Sarah and the children, Xavier went upstairs to the room, removed his clothes, and got in bed. The room was dark, and, while his eyes adjusted, within the depth of that darkness he believed he saw things—the shape of a man standing at the foot of the bed.

Xavier closed his eyes, heard Sarah or one of the kids coming up the stairs, and when he opened them again the apparition was gone. *What does Caledonia know that I don't?* he thought.

Sarah entered the room, but didn't turn on the light. She moved toward the bed, sat down, and felt her husband's head with her lukewarm hand.

"Are you all right?" she asked.

"Been feeling a little dizzy."

"Get some sleep, all right?" she said. "I want to stay up with the children for a while. We'll talk tomorrow."

Sarah left and closed the door.

A cold sweat awoke Xavier in the middle of the night. His skin felt moist, as if he'd been running a high fever. He sat up as carefully as possible so as not to wake his wife. Sliding out of bed, his feet touched the cold tile of the floor. He shivered. The cold sensation immediately worked on his bladder. Feeling the pressure, he quickly tiptoed from the bedroom and into the bathroom. After he urinated, Xavier stood in front of the sink and checked his face in the mirror. Nothing unusual about the way he looked: sleepy and tired, that was all.

Through the bathroom window, which was cracked open, came the sound of the torrential rains falling hard against everything in the darkened back yard. Trees, plants, grass, mud...the frogs croaked. The sounds grew louder and louder. Croaking, chirping, buzzing...

It was out of these nocturnal sounds that Xavier thought he heard the voice emerge.

Your quest is a simple one, the voice said.

At this moment Xavier's choices became very limited. If he ran back into the bedroom and startled Sarah awake and told her what was going on, she'd suspect what she probably suspected all along, that he was crazy. But Xavier wasn't schizophrenic, and the voice he heard was certainly not that of his imagination. Or was it?

No, this voice spoke out to him. *I can help you.*

Was it the spirit guide? Xavier thought and stood as quiet as possible. He was confused, not wanting to believe the voice he was hearing.

This is certainly no time for doubt. Look at it this way, man. The way I see it, I can really make a difference in your life.

He didn't know what to say, since he didn't believe any of this was happening. *This is all too fast for me*, Xavier answered in his mind finally.

We've got all the time in the world.

I don't understand. He could hear the voice, but where was it coming from?

If I had your troubles, I wouldn't have your troubles. All you have to do is go back. By going back, you'll figure things out for yourself. One lifetime's all we have.

All this happened that same day after Caledonia had seen Xavier. Now, something in Xavier was set astir.

He twisted open the sink faucet and splashed cold water over his face, but the voice was still there.

Things can't change for you, the spirit said, until you go back.

Go back where?

Reexamine your predicament.

The croaking of the frogs came from very far away, from deep in the banks of the canal and the neighbors' back yards.

All you have to do is listen.

Xavier sat on the plastic lid of the toilet and buried his face in his hands. He thought about his comfortable life, his wife sound asleep in the bedroom, his two children in their rooms down the hall. *Comfortable*, he contemplated, *and in the end what did it all mean?*

Snap out of it.

Everything's gone wrong. Way too wrong. He was shivering.

You want to know what your problem is? said the spirit. Then there was a long moment of silence. Xavier stared at the see-through plastic shower curtains. The white tiles behind it seemed to glow, as if struck by moonlight.

The spirit continued, *You expect too much. Sooner or later you're going to have to start taking it easy. Relax. Enjoy yourself a little more. You have to go back to the beginning. You have to come in contact with your old self. Think back. Remember how you were before things became cluttered. See through the fog. Clear your mind. Only when you return to basics will you find new meaning in your life. Peace and understanding.*

I don't believe any of this, said Xavier. *This is a joke.*

You must believe. What were you expecting anyway, out of your life I mean?

Not much, Xavier answered, *a little happiness…*

And you don't have that?

Not enough.

That's because it is in your nature to be dissatisfied. You have high expectations. You demand too much from yourself. Good qualities, but not in excess. As I've told you already, you need to dig deeper and bring forth some other part of you. One that is less careful and more carefree.

That was easy to say, hard to do.

I'll help you as much as I can.

Sleep's what I need. I need to rest. Xavier was willing to bet that if he slept well tonight, the following day all this would seem like a dream.

Let me help you.

All right, whatever…

You have nothing to lose.

I have my troubles.

Stay tuned and listen…

Was he imagining the voice, Xavier thought as he sat on the toilet seat, face cradled in his hands, and listened to the spirit.

Something was wrong. The voice stopped. The etherial humdrum of the rain drops falling outside replaced the silence. There was a knock on the door.

"Xavier."

It was Sarah.

"Are you okay?"

"I'm fine," he said. He leaned against the door and listened for her footsteps, in case she returned to the bed.

"I need to use the bathroom."

"Out in a sec," he said.

He waited in the bathroom for the voice to return, but nothing happened. All he heard were the drops of rain falling on the leaves outside. Xavier opened the door and let Sarah in. She looked sleepy, the lines from the sheets marked on her face. He expected her to ask what he'd been doing all that time, but she stepped into the bathroom and closed the door. For an instant he felt confused, not knowing whether to wait for Sarah to finish so he could go back in or climb into bed and forget everything and go to sleep.

Sarah flushed the toilet and opened the door. She found Xavier standing there in the dark. "What's the matter?" she asked. "Come to bed."

"I can't sleep," he told her.

She knows, he thought. He walked to the bed and sat down. Then he felt strange, as light as a feather. He fell back on the mattress. Involuntarily, he turned to face Sarah.

I promise to help you, said the spirit. *To start with you need some tender loving care...*

Xavier rolled over on top of Sarah and kissed her. His hands searched under her nighty for her breasts. Her nipples stood firm and hardened against his touch. As he pushed against her pelvis, his penis became erect.

"What's come over you?" she said, and caught her breath.

He unbuttoned her nighty and kissed her breasts. He bit her nipples. Sarah moaned. "We'll wake up the children," she said.

"They can't hear us," he said, and went down her stomach. He circled her belly button with his tongue, then pushed her pants down. He moved on the bed, low enough to sink his face, nose and mouth into the moist soft flesh between her legs.

Sarah held on to his head as if she thought she'd have to guide him.

"Is it the sex?" he said, breathing in deep and hard.

"What?"

"What is it?" he asked again. "Is it the sex?"

"No," she said. "It's not the sex. Don't stop."

This you call problems?

Xavier and Sarah made love as they had not done in a long time. Xavier for a moment forgot about his anxiety and frustrations.

He came hard and then moved off Sarah.

Sarah turned to him and reminded him that she was leaving with the children that afternoon for Illinois. Her parents, who were always dying to see their grandchildren, would be happy indeed, she said, and stretched.

"Tell me what is..." Xavier began to say, but changed his mind. His heart was racing.

"What?" she said. "Tell me, what's on your mind?"

"Nothing," he concluded. "I just want to know what you think the problem with us is."

"Maybe it's me," she said. "I need to get away for a while."

There was a deep silence now, then Sarah broke it: "Francesca called."

"Who?"

"You remember Francesca," she said. "My voice teacher in Tucson. We housesat for her one winter."

He remembered vaguely. Ah, yes, Francesca and that neurotic cat of hers. The Persian cat—what was his name?—kept throwing up hairballs, and, because he only liked being around his owner, shitting all over the carpet. What a week that was at Francesca's. *Fluffy?*

"What did she say?"

"She's directing in New York. She has a small part she thinks I'm perfect for."

"Small part?"

"Are you kidding," Sarah said. "It's a beginning. It's something. See, you don't understand."

"I understand," he said, "but you're going to Illinois, not New York."

"I'm leaving the children with my parents," she said. "I'm going to try New York."

"Don't go now," he said. "If you go now, I won't be able to go with you."

"I don't want you to come with us."

"All this work."

"Did you hear? I said I don't want you to come. It's better if you don't."

"Lindy's birthday's coming up."

"She wants to go to Illinois."

"We can take her this summer."

"It *is* summer," said Sarah. "School's been over for a few weeks."

"So what's going to happen?"

Silence again.

"Are you coming back?" he asked.

"I don't know," she said. "I told you I need time."

Sarah rolled over on her side, her back to Xavier.

This is crazy, he thought. "I have to think about this," he said.

"I've already thought about it too long," she said.

Xavier closed his eyes. His mouth felt parched, his lips dry.

Things get worse before they get better.

Eventually he fell asleep and dreamt. He dreamt of millions of frogs, all sizes, emerging out of the canal and filling up his back yard. Brandy, loose in the yard, suddenly found herself cornered. The frogs attacked her. A bullfrog spat at her face and blinded her. Brandy's howls took on a human quality, evolved into a voice of despair and painful agony. This became the horror of Xavier's dream, that Brandy's voice was his own. When the inevitable was about to happen, that the frogs would turn carnivorous and eat Brandy, a faceless man appeared from some unseen place and saved the dog. The man stood there and petted Brandy. The dog licked his hands.

Every problem has a solution.

Next morning they ate breakfast together. Corn flakes and low-fat milk for everyone. The children ate quickly and fought over the prize in the new cereal box. Sarah broke up the argument. Nobody was in any mood to talk after that. The kids looked at each other and then at their father. Xavier reached over and stuck his hand into the cereal box. He searched until he found the plastic-wrapped surprise. He pulled his hand out and showed it to the kids.

"Stickers," said Xavier, and bit the wrapper off. He gave one sticker to each kid.

"You guys ready to fly?" Xavier asked.

"They're not stickers, Dad," Eric said. "Tattoos."

"Wow," said Lindy.

"Visit Grandma and Grandpa in Illinois?"

Eric slapped his tattoo on his forearm and held it there.

"Are you guys listening to me?" asked Xavier.

"Cool," said Eric.

"I like mine," said Lindy.

"Hey," Xavier told them, "you guys listening?"

Both children looked at him as if he'd interrupted their fun.

"You guys ready to go?"

"Sure," said Eric, and returned his attention to the tattoo.

"I'll miss you," Xavier said to Lindy, who was trying to get the thing on her forearm, too.

"Grandma has a surprise for us," said Eric.

"For me," said Lindy. "It's my birthday."

"She'll have one for each of you," Sarah cut in.

"What time is the flight leaving?" Xavier asked Sarah.

"Three this afternoon."

"I'll pick you guys up and take you."

The airport wasn't too far away. Sarah told Xavier not to forget to pick up a gift for Lindy, something to open after she blew out the candles on her cake. Remembering to buy a gift was not the hard part. The hard part was for Xavier to find the time to do all the things he needed to do.

"Back to work?" Sarah asked him.

"I have to."

"You feel ready?"

"Ready as I'll ever feel."

The phone rang then and he got up to answer it. It was Wilfredo. He was in the office. "A client called," he told Xavier.

"Not Segovia, right?"

"No, everything's cool with him."

"Who was it then?"

"Eloísa," Wilfredo said. "She needs for you to call her A. S. A. P."

"Did she say what for?"

"Nope."

There was the sound of paper being crumpled on the line.

"Want me to pick you up?" Wilfredo asked.

"Thanks, but I'll drive," Xavier said.

"Back in business."

Xavier hung up and got his things. The kids still sat at the table. They showed off their tattoos to each other. He kissed them and said goodbye to them and Sarah.

As soon as he arrived at the office, Xavier called Caledonia. Again Fabiola answered the phone and he asked to speak to the *Santísima*.

Shortly after, Caledonia spoke to him on the line. She told him she didn't have too much free time.

"It'll only take a minute."

"*Dímelo*," she said.

"Who's the spirit?"

"He hasn't spoken to you?"

"He has, but I don't know his name."

"Sonny Manteca."

"Who's that?"

"A musician."

Xavier smiled because he still didn't believe in this stuff. He knew it was entirely possible that she was helping him make it all up.

"What else do you need to know?" asked Caledonia.

"That's it."

"So long then," she said. "Good luck."

They hung up.

Wilfredo walked in with a couple of *pastelitos de guayaba*. "Have one," Wilfredo said to Xavier, and showed him the guayaba-filled pastries.

"Do you know who Sonny Manteca is?"

"You kidding?" Wilfredo asked, and bit one of the pastries in half. He wiped the crumbs off his mouth with the back of his hand.

"No, who is he?"

"He's a *Cubiche*." Cubiche meant he was Cuban.

"But what else? What else do you know about him?"

"He is…" Wilfredo swallowed. "Was a Cuban conga player. Possibly the best. C'mon, man, you've heard of Sonny Manteca. Who hasn't?"

"What happened to him? Do you know that?"

"He's dead. I know that much. But he left us some fine music. I think I've got some at the apartment."

Xavier ate his pastry and reclined on the chair.

"No more spontaneous emotional combustions, okay?" Wilfredo said, and smiled.

Xavier told his partner how his father had taken him to see Caledonia and about the spirit she summoned and how he didn't know if he was supposed to believe any of that stuff.

"That's heavy duty," Wilfredo said.

"Do you believe it?" Xavier asked.

"About the powers? Sure."

"I'm not sure I do."

"Whatever happens," he said, "I think you'll be fine."

"I don't know."

"You'll see," he said in an isn't-it-nice-to-be-alive-this-morning tone of voice that rubbed Xavier the wrong way. "All you need is a little R & R."

Xavier confided in Wilfredo all the things that had been happening, including Xavier's hearing the voice.

"So," said Wilfredo, "listen, go with it. What have you got to lose?"

Wilfredo smiled and looked into Xavier's eyes. He thought his office partner would soon get over this.

"Right now I have a crazy urge," Xavier said.

"What's that?"

"Buy the finest set of congas. Practice and learn how to play."

"Sure, play the congas. That can be relaxing."

"No, I need to convince myself that I can do something other than sell insurance."

Wilfredo told his partner about how well he played soccer, that he wasn't a one-trick pony. "You have to accept what you are, man."

What am I? Xavier thought and then asked, "What is that?"

Wilfredo started this long harangue about being like an iguana, which, as he defined it, was a person who needed to blend, camouflage in order to fit in.

"You mean chameleon," Xavier tried to clarify.

"Iguana, chameleon, what's the difference?"

"One uses camouflage, the other..."

"See, that's the problem with you," he said. "Forget technicalities. Go with the flow. Stop analyzing..."

Leave these crossroads.

A person needed to blend in, Wilfredo continued, or the worse was to be expected: the individual lost himself.

Xavier was amazed. "Soccer was a long time ago. I need something to bring back my confidence. Take my mind off things."

"Do it," he said. "Let this voice guide you."

Xavier told him that Sarah was leaving for Illinois with the kids, and that he didn't have too much time to spend in the office.

"For good," he said.

"What?"

"Is she leaving? Leaving you?"

Xavier thought about it, then answered, "I don't know."

"It wouldn't surprise me," Wilfredo said.

"What does that mean?"

"You guys have had your troubles from the beginning. We've talked about this before. Oil and vinegar don't mix. Maybe you knew it was coming. You've known all along and that's your problem now."

"You're crazy," Xavier told him.

"Anyway," he said, "you can take more time off. I can handle the office. The Segovia thing's under control. Your father came through with the money."

Wilfredo, Xavier understood, made sense. No reason to make a big deal about the present situation. *But the present situation, my present situation, is all there is!*

"I know this music store," Wilfredo said. "That's if you really want the congas."

Years earlier, when Xavier and Sarah separated before Lindy was born, Wilfredo and Xavier lived together. It was really more Wilfredo's idea than his that they share a one-bedroom apartment. Wilfredo, the eternal bachelor. In those days they worked together, lived together, ate together. Needless to say the arrangement quickly turned ugly.

Xavier became weary of Wilfredo's sexual escapades. Where did he get all the energy? He went about dating,

Xavier thought, the way hunters go after wild geese: with fervor and absolute determination. With tenacity. Women came and went out of the apartment. If they were to be "repeats," they would most likely have their own key. And all the time Xavier kept asking himself: What about Wilfredo brought women to this jungle of shag carpets and colorful furniture? Was it his friendliness? Was it his sense of humor? His eyes? Smile? The hairs on his chest? What? But, as always, Wilfredo found someone.

If Wilfredo returned late in the night or in the early morning, Xavier, who slept in the bedroom, would be awakened by the ooohs and aaahs of love-making or by midnight runs to the bathroom or refrigerator. Never before had he heard the springs of a sofa bed squeak so loudly! Xavier was beginning to suspect that his friend and partner possessed a large member. Or one with some kind of deformity. A wart. A mole. A tattoo. Who knew? A hooked penis?

Often, Wilfredo talked Xavier into going out to a club with him. So Xavier got to know the club scene in Miami over one summer. Going out to night clubs every night took its toll. For a while Xavier became a *murcielago*, a bat, which was what Wilfredo called a person who partied every night. He *was* like a vampire, no doubt. The lifestyle, anyway. Loved the night and hated the mornings. Mornings meant work for Wilfredo—the stake finally driven through the heart of his fun. Party over. Monday morning meant the worse of all fates: the beginning of the workweek. Whereas Xavier found Monday mornings to be his favorite: back on the job with lots to do. Stuff to keep his mind busy. A new chance to out-do himself, his sales. A new chance to procure clients, impress people.

One night Xavier returned to the apartment with an ex-cop, ex-wife, ex-girlfriend, ex, ex, ex, from New York. What followed turned out to be the most sordid night of Xavier's life. This woman asked him to piss on her and Xavier couldn't do it. Hit her? Couldn't do it. Bite her? He tried. Harder. Couldn't do it.

The following morning, Xavier hated himself, promised he'd never have another one-night stand. By the end of the summer, when Xavier and Sarah started the Lamaze classes, Xavier wasted little time reconciling with his wife.

They drove to a music store on Ponce de Leon Avenue on the other side of Coral Gables and got there ten minutes before it opened. There was a cafeteria at the corner, so they went in and had some coffee.

"I'm not Cuban enough," Xavier said.

"What do you mean?" asked Wilfredo. Then, "You were the one who at one time felt too submerged in the culture. You hate Hialeah."

"Don't hate it," he said. "It's the people I no longer understand."

"What's to understand? The folks live in their own little reality. They live and die here with hopes of one day going back. They're just waiting."

"Do you ever wish you could go back?"

"Not really. What would I go back for? My family's here."

"A way of life," said Xavier.

"A way of life is a way of life. We live here, fuck here, and die here—that's a way of life, too."

"I don't feel Cuban anymore. Not as much as I feel American."

"You are neither, bro."

"No, I don't buy that iguana thing you talk about."

"There's nothing you can do about it," he said. "Besides, it comes automatic. You've *been* doing it."

"There's got to be a better way," Xavier added, and drank his murky, creamed coffee. "We've spent more time in this country than in the other. Three-fourths of our lives. Now I am feeling the disconnection. There's been a clean and clear break. I can feel it."

"Those are the blues," Wilfredo said. "It'll pass."

The crossroads…

"Something tells me otherwise."

"We're all in the same predicament, bro, and there's no sense in thinking about it. You do the best you can and move on, you know what I mean? Life's too short."

By now the store had opened, so they finished the rest of their coffee and left. The minute Xavier stepped inside the store, he felt as though a child, not him, had walked into a toy store. He thought *percussion*. Immediately, they walked over to the drums, where, in the corner, they found what he'd been looking for: a set of congas.

Wilfredo called out for help. A salesman, a chubby, red-cheeked middle-aged man left his place behind the desk and joined Xavier and Wilfredo by the congas.

"You're looking at the best of the best."

"What are they made of?"

"Plexiglas."

"Plexiglas?"

"Yeah, fiberglass reinforced plastic," the salesman maintained, "has the same tonality as the Cuban skins."

For me, it's wood or nothing. "They look too high tech."

"Ah, but they sound good nonetheless."

Xavier wasn't convinced. Then the salesman, who was Cuban-American too, told them about Cuban-made congas or *tumbadoras*, as they were called, which were carved from a solid block of cedar or mahogany and topped by drumheads made of goat skin. "They weighed a ton," said the salesman, "but nothing like their sound."

"Do you have any like that?" asked Xavier.

"Not new," he said. "I have a used pair in the back. You want to see them?"

Xavier told the salesman to lead the way. In the storage room, the salesman opened two boxes and brought the congas out. They were huge. One was painted green and the other yellow.

"Go ahead and test them if you like."

Xavier placed the palm of his hand on the soft surface.

He found a chair by a humming water fountain, brought it over to the congas and sat down. Wilfredo looked at his partner in awe. Xavier grabbed the congas,

positioned them between his legs and felt the smooth sur-
face of their skins. He could tell the male from the female,
the baja from the alta, by touch.

Luckily there were no other customers except for Wil-
fredo and Xavier, and Wilfredo wasn't buying. Xavier
began to play. He played as if he were playing in front of
a large audience. Both Wilfredo and the salesman stared
with bewildered smiles on their faces. They couldn't
believe the sound; Xavier couldn't believe it himself. Boy,
could he bang on those congas. He kept a steady, exuber-
ant beat. The drumming went: truc, trac-truc, tricky-
ticky, trac-tac, tuc-tuc!

Some of the people inside a cubicle office came out to
listen.

"Who is this guy?" the salesman asked Wilfredo.

"An insurance agent."

The salesman looked at Wilfredo and smiled.

Outside, people stopped to listen to the sound. As if
hypnotized, they stood by the door and windows and lis-
tened. Some couldn't help but dance.

"Test them," the salesman said. "Go ahead."

"These are the ones," Xavier said. "We'll take them."

Xavier felt the excitement in his blood. Perhaps this
would make the difference. It was the sudden realization
that something as easy as playing the congas could
make him feel so good. Giddy with pleasure, Xavier paid
for the instruments and took them to the office.

As they dropped off the congas, Xavier remembered
the time and that he had to take his family to the airport. Also, he needed to get a gift for Lindy. So he and
Wilfredo drove to a toy store and bought Lindy a teddy

bear. It was beige and had a big red bow around its neck. Its smile and large happy eyes would make Lindy's day. The teddy was so big that Xavier was afraid that they weren't going to let Lindy on the plane with it.

Xavier made it to the house on time. Lindy was so happy with her gift that she made Eric ride up front on Wilfredo's lap because she wanted the bear in the back seat with her. Wilfredo came along to the airport and helped with the luggage. At the gate, Xavier took turns hugging his family. Lindy could hardly carry the bear, which the man at the gate let her carry on.

After he said goodbye to Eric and Lindy, Sarah hugged and kissed Xavier. She told him to get plenty of rest, that she'd call as soon as she got to her parent's house. She also said goodbye to Wilfredo. After they boarded the plane and the plane was pulled away from the terminal, Xavier and Wilfredo returned to the office. They took the congas to Xavier's house and put them in the garage.

It was there where Xavier sat down and practiced on the congas, played and didn't return to work...

Ever hear of contrapunteo?

Musical rhythms that can't be written down because no one knows how, but they're there, these subtle and not so subtle insinuations of beat and tone, surging, coming up through the beat, constantly mixing and layering.

Why can't I be Cuban here?

Because geography matters. Geography and climate matter. This is what I'm talking about. You've lost your way because you've become a bland mix of nothing but routines. Thoughtless, meaningless routines. This is the American way. You don't want to do this. Life here has no rhythm, only empty chores. Right?

He played and didn't stop to eat the Chinese food Wilfredo ordered...

Why is Wilfredo happy?

What makes you think he is? Look at him. He's nothing but a cultural opportunist. No responsibilities to speak of. For him chasing after women is his aimless routine. Wake up, for being Cuban isn't about being a member of some elite group or community. It is about dealing with the life you were dealt. A certain way of life, filled with tropical and cultural rhythms, but since you are living here, that doesn't exist.

Where is the salsa? The sabor? The zest?

Not here. Life here is a void.

So what's the answer?

Go back...go back to where you belong, your rightful place in time. Our history, your history, is one of returning...

He played until the nextdoor neighbors came across the lawn and knocked on the door and complained about the noise...

What about my life here?

What about it? Has it been in vain? No, it hasn't, but it hasn't been the life you would have led. In a sense it has been a fake, a trick of circumstances. In short, you've been living the wrong life.

He played until the neighbors called the cops and they came and told Xavier to stop making so much racket...

This is only an attempt to heal you, make you whole again, balance the Cuban, eradicate this Cuban-American thing. You need to return to essentials. Simplify your life. Regain your spiritual cultural connection. When was the last time you ate the food (vaca frita, ropa vieja, moros, yuca con mojo, maduros?), danced to the music. (You don't know how to dance, do you? And if you did at one time, you've probably forgotten), live the life of a Cuban waiting, waiting for his land to be free.

Might be waiting a long time.

The point is you need to reconnect.

He played after the cops left, and finally played until late in the evening when Sarah called to say they had made it to her parent's okay. Wilfredo, sleepy and tired and with a splitting headache, dragged Xavier out of the garage and closed the door.

It was then and only then that Xavier was able to rest.

Xavier remembered the trip to Sarah's parents'. He found himself sitting next to Sarah on the very front seat of the bus behind the driver who, from Tucson to El Paso, chewed tobacco and spat into a styrofoam cup. An old woman sat behind them, repeating, "I will take my cars and clothes and take them to the Salvation Army. He'll see." This became a litany. She chained-smoked, so the driver told her to go to the back of the bus. Probably some woman getting divorced, he thought. It seemed like everybody in the world was getting divorced—his parents were—so why would anybody get married?

Shortly before they arrived at the station in El Paso, where they were supposed to change buses, the woman returned, sat behind them, then reached over and tapped Xavier on the shoulder.

"Do you read the Bible?" she asked. "The Psalms?"

"Read them all," he told the woman, and this made Sarah laugh so hard she hid her face. The woman left them alone after that, and they slept leaning against each other.

Her parents waited for them at the station in Peoria. He couldn't guess who they were in the crowd of people there until this couple approached Sarah from behind. Xavier stood back while they took turns hugging and kissing their daughter.

Her father was a tall, white-haired, broad-shouldered man. He took Xavier's hand and eyed him over. Xavier didn't like the red and blue veins on the tip of his nose. Mrs. Triste took Xavier's hand into her mittened hands and shook it. She didn't let go right away; instead she held them and told him how utterly wonderful it was to make his acquaintance.

She had a small, round face, yellowish hair which hid under the hood of her coat, pudgy nose, lips the color of frozen meant.

"Happy to meet you," he said.

Snow covered the ground up to their ankles outside the bus station.

Sarah's mother told them to get inside the car, that they were going to a restaurant for dinner. Feeling tired, dirty from the two days without a shower, Xavier sat in the back of the Buick Regal and rested his tired eyes. He was tired from seeing so much of America's heartland.

They arrived at the restaurant and Mrs. Triste was still talking about John Deere shutting down their plant. "A lot of people are leaving Peoria," she said, "and a lot of them come to Pat for counseling."

Sarah's father was a marriage counselor, Ph.D. in Psychology. And her mother taught at a school for the mentally handicapped.

The conversation continued over dinner. Xavier quickly ate his sirloin steak and mashed potatoes. Mr. Triste wasn't saying much. Mrs. Triste asked him where his parents lived.

"They're divorced," he said.

An opera enthusiast like his daughter, Mr. Triste started talking about what a terrible fate young Italian boys who were sopranos had in the eighteenth century. "Castrati sopranos," he said.

"Castrated sopranos?" Xavier asked.

Mrs. Triste and Sarah smiled, but Mr. Triste grew serious.

Patrick Triste didn't like him, Xavier thought—not good enough for his daughter.

Dinner over, they drove to the house, a two-story, four-bedroom place. They had bought it cheap and planned to restore and remodel most of it by the next summer. Xavier was glad to be getting out of the cold.

Mrs. Triste made hot chocolate and served it on the dining room table under which the wooden waxed floors shone. Mr. Triste grew tired and said he was turning in.

"Make yourself at home here," was what Mrs. Triste said to him before she left. To Sarah, she said, "Sarah, honey, show him to his room downstairs. Get a fire going in the fireplace if he wants. If not, get the portable heater out of the closet."

"I'll take care of him, Mother," Sarah said.

Her mother said good night and left.

"I want to go to sleep," Xavier said.

"Party pooper."

Sarah led him downstairs to what was to be his bedroom, started a fire in the fireplace, placed the screen in front of the flames, and fixed his bed.

"He doesn't like me," Xavier told her.

"Who? My father?"

"Did you see the way he kept looking at me?"

"He looks at everybody like that."

"I don't know..." Xavier said.

"You're crazy," she said, kissed him good night and left.

After dinner the following night, Mr. Triste asked Xavier to accompany him outside to get more wood for the fireplace. The cold snuck in through the cuffs of Xavier's shrink-to-fit Levi's and made him shudder as he followed Mr. Triste to the wood pile.

"It's *J*avier, isn't it? Not *X*avier. Like Mexico is Me*j*i-co," Mr. Triste said, and brushed the snow off.

"X-avier," Xavier said.

Mr. Triste picked up a couple of logs and handed them to Xavier.

"Never been in this kind of weather, Xavier?" he asked.

"I prefer warmth," he told the man.

Mr. Triste stood still for a moment, breath smoking out of his mouth. "We want Sarah to return here after she graduates," he said, and put a couple of more logs on Xavier's arms.

"She plans to go to Miami and take voice lessons," Xavier said.

"And you plan to follow her?"

"I'm from there."

"There's something you should know," Mr. Triste said. "Both of you need to stop and think about this. Long and hard. You both need to realize that it's going to be tough."

Xavier asked him what he meant by "tough."

"You come from a different world than she does," he said, "and you're bound to have disagreements. Lots of them."

This made Xavier angry, so he told Mr. Triste, "Sarah's a woman now, Mr. Triste. I think she knows what she wants."

"Do *you* know what you want?"

"I believe so."

Mr. Triste walked back to the house in silence. Xavier followed him, his feet sinking into the snow as he carried the logs. Inside, Mr. Triste took the logs from him and stacked them by the fireplace. Then he washed his hands in the kitchen and went to his room.

The next morning Sarah woke Xavier up. "Hey, sleepyhead," she said, and kissed him. "I have a surprise for you." She walked over to the stereo. "We have the house all to ourselves," she said, searching through the records.

She found the one she was looking for and put it on the turntable.

Sarah removed her terry-cloth robe and dropped it on the rug. "Listen," she said, "and make love to me."

Wagner's "Ride of the Valkyries" started. It was loud. "I don't feel comfortable doing this," Xavier said.

While they screwed, Mr. Triste stood in the doorway, red in the face. Sarah saw her father and blushed. She pushed Xavier off and stood up.

Mr. Triste went upstairs.

Feeling a little dizzy, Xavier stood and watched Sarah put on her robe. "Jesus," she said, "fuck! We had our asses to the door. He saw it all."

She rushed out of the room and he heard her go upstairs.

"I want him out," Mr. Triste said. "That son of a bitch."

"It's my fault," she pleaded to no avail.

Xavier felt like going upstairs and apologizing, but what good was it to say that he was sorry? There was nothing left to do but pack and get out of the house.

Sarah returned, saw him packing, sat on the bed and didn't say a word.

"Drive me to the airport," he told her. "I'll catch the next flight out."

"I'm sorry," she said.

"Bad luck," he said. "Maybe if I talked with him."

"That won't change how he feels. We've betrayed him," she said.

"Let me talk to him."

"You've got to go back to Tucson."

"I'm sorry," Xavier said. This was the last thing he said to Sarah, then she drove him to the airport and he flew back to the desert.

After that, once she returned and they planned to stay together, her parents cut her off for a long time. That was what made them decide to return to Miami. Besides, by then Xavier had damaged his knee and ruined his chances of playing pro. By then, Sarah was pregnant with Eric.

The next morning Xavier felt drained. He came downstairs in his underwear. Barefoot, he felt the cold kitchen tiles and suddenly wanted to take a piss. He didn't know where the bathroom was, so he held it. As he squatted to look for food in the cupboards, the need seemed to go away.

Lindy's fish swam slowly in the bowl, rose for a gulp of air, and sank to the bottom. *He'll need to eat*, Xavier thought, *but where is the food?*

Brandy was asleep on her cushion. Her stomach rose and fell with each breath.

Am I hungry? He looked through the cabinets, *for what?* He didn't know. There were canned goods galore and cereal boxes and jars. The glasses and coffee mugs were upside down—that's why they always had that vinegary smell. There was nothing in the kitchen he wanted to eat. The refrigerator was empty except for things he'd have to cook up, and he didn't know how to cook anything.

There was a knock on the door. Brandy perked up and ran out of the kitchen. She barked at whomever it was standing outside. Xavier walked into the living room, picked up the dog, and cradled her in his arms. Brandy shivered and kicked her legs.

Xavier opened the door just as he was: barefoot and in his underwear.

Two young people dressed in blue slacks and white pullovers stood there. The young woman, a big orange bow in her blonde hair, looked at him and blushed.

"Hello, sir," said the young man. Short hair and tan. "We were passing through the neighborhood and...we wonder if you have a minute?"

"Stranded?" Xavier asked.

"No, sir," the young man said. "We'd like a moment of your time.'

Then Xavier looked down and saw what they carried: Bibles and pamphlets.

"Sir," the young woman said, "a moment of your time?"

"As you can see…" Xavier said, and paused.

A garbage truck roared by, passed the house, and turned right at the next street.

"Don't have much time," Xavier continued.

Brandy growled.

"It'll only take a sec."

"Maybe we can come by later," she said.

The young man reached out with a pamphlet in hand.

"What is it?" Xavier asked, not taking.

"You might want to read it soon," the girl said.

Xavier looked at the cover of the pamphlet. It was a blond and blue-eyed Jesus posing a la Uncle Sam. The bold print read: I CAN SAVE YOU.

Xavier refused to take the pamphlet. The young man held it out to Xavier until his hand began to shake.

"Sorry," Xavier said finally, and closed the door.

The young man shouted: "YOU CAN'T BE SAVED IF YOU DON'T ACCEPT JESUS CHRIST AS YOUR SAVIOR!"

Xavier stood there and held Brandy until he heard them leave. Then he released Brandy, who went back to the kitchen, curled up on her cushion and yawned as she put her head down.

Selling for a living. No more of that.

The silence of the empty house grew to be too much, so he hurried.

He drank a glass of water and then hurried upstairs to go to the bathroom.

The phone ran several times.

"Hell-o"

"Mrs. Triste," he said, "this is Xavier."

"Xavier," she said, "how are you?"

He heard the sound of the TV in the background. He leaned against the bedroom wall and said, "I was just calling to see..."

"Hold on, Xavier," she said.

There was a lot of static on the line and then the sound of the TV in the background stopped. Mrs. Triste came back on. "Sorry," she said, "I had the news on too loud."

"Is Sarah there?" he asked.

"No, she's gone out."

"And the children?"

"Pat took them to the movies."

Silence.

"Should I have her call you?"

"No, I'll call her later."

"I'm sure she'll be back in no time."

"Okay, thanks."

They hung up.

The deepest silence engulfed him. Suddenly Xavier thought of the distance and the time change and how he'd never belong, not with them, not here.

Eloísa got through to Xavier. Initially he didn't recognize the voice and, when he did, he wanted to hang up.

"*Muchacho*," she said. "You don't know what I've been through. The last few days have been a nightmare."

Who's she talking to? Don't I know it, he thought.

He stayed on the line, bracing himself for the bad news. "Izquierdo?" he asked.

"He passed away," she said, and succumbed to silence.

Grief.

"I'm sorry," he said.

He heard Eloísa's attempt at composure, the wiping of the skin under her eyes, the blowing of her nose.

"He..." she started to say, then blew her nose one final time. "He left something for you."

"Please..."

"A box. He instructed me to tell you to either come by and pick it up or for me to take it to your office."

"I'll pick it up," he said.

"I can ride the bus out there," she said.

"No need to do that. I'll pick it up."

"He wanted you to have them."

Them? he thought. He didn't want to be rude and ask what *they* were.

"When can you come by?"

"Tomorrow morning," he said.

"I'll be here," she said.

"Is there anything you need?"

"No, I'm fine. I'm just so alone now."

He was talking on the kitchen phone. He saw the layer of bubbles on the surface of Lindy's fish bowl.

"You know," she said, "Izquierdo respected you so much."

The fish moved and Xavier exhaled.

"He was a good man," Xavier said.

"He often said you were the most serious and dedicated young man he knew."

Xavier didn't know what else to say. "So I'll come by tomorrow."

"*Adiós*," she said, and hung up.

He dialed his mother's number. The phone rang and then a man answered, "Hello..."

Xavier couldn't say anything, but he also found he couldn't hang up.

"*¡Oigo!*" the man said. "Hello."

Xavier hung up fast.

In the afternoon he received a call from Sarah.

"The kids are fine," she said. "Having a great time."

"Tomorrow's Lindy's birthday, isn't it?" he asked.

"It sure is."

"The house feels strange without you guys." ·

"Listen," she said, and paused as if she were looking for a little privacy. "I've decided to go on to New York. I can't pass up this opportunity. I'd be crazy."

"And the kids?"

"They're fine here," she said. "I've already spoken to my parents. They don't mind."

"How long?..."

"That I don't know."

"There's nothing I can say?" he asked.

"No."

"Nothing I can do to change your mind?"

"My mind's made up."

"So you won't be coming back?"

"I didn't say that," she said. "But I don't know when."

"Good luck," he told her, and hung up.

Xavier stood in the dining room when he heard the sound of the lawn mower. He remembered he needed to pay Benito, the yardman. He walked out of the house and found Benito pushing the lawn mower toward the back yard.

Benito pushed along and made a straight line. He was a short man, bowlegged, who'd come to the United States through the port of Mariel, Cuba.

On the way back to the front, Benito and Xavier made eye contact. Benito wore, as always, his protective goggles. It made his small face look out of proportion, frog-like.

Xavier reached for his wallet.

Benito released the throttle and the machine quieted down.

Xavier looked at him and said in Spanish, "What do you think of me, Benito?" He handed the man the money, which Benito took and without counting it shoved deep into his shirt pocket.

Benito looked at Xavier, squinted behind the goggles. "I don't understand," he said.

"*¿Como me ves?*" How do you see me?

"Ah," said Benito, and smiled. "*Hombre*, you look good. Healthy. You live in this nice house. In good neighborhood. Drive fancy car. Beautiful wife. Good children. You've made your way in this country. You are a lucky man."

Then Benito pulled on the throttle and gave the lawn mower gas.

Xavier stood by as Benito turned around and continued with the mowing.

Xavier called his father, but there was no answer. He dialed his mother and again a man answered. Xavier thought he knew who the man was, but didn't speak to him. "Must be some idiot," the man said, and hung up.

He drove out to Wilfredo's place. Wilfredo lived in the Gables, too, but way on the other side in apartment row. Xavier drove by the parking lot and spotted his partner's Camaro. He parked next to it, locked the car, and went up the stairs.

He knocked several times and then he heard the footsteps approach, and then the door opened. Wilfredo stood there wearing a bathrobe. His hair was wet.

"In the shower?"

Wilfredo looked at him and said, "Hey, X, I've got company."

"I'll come by later," Xavier told him.

"Are you okay?" Wilfredo asked.

"Sure," Xavier told him, "I just wanted to know if you wanted to go out for dinner."

"You know I would, but..." Wilfredo looked at Xavier and winked.

"I understand," Xavier said.

"Maybe later. Will you be home?"

"After I eat."

"I'll call you."

"Have fun," Xavier told him, and walked away.

"Always," Wilfredo said, and closed the door.

Trying to avoid returning to the office, Xavier drove around for a place to eat. Fast-food joints everywhere, but he didn't want to eat any of that stuff tonight. Tonight he craved something different, so he drove up through Calle Ocho, past Caledonia's. There was a line of people outside waiting to get in and he wondered why. He stared at the people in the rearview mirror after he passed, looked on so long he didn't realize it when he ran a red light.

He drove on and decided to eat at La Carreta, a Cuban restaurant that had been at this location for as long as he could remember. They called it the cart because the restaurant's façade was that of a giant oxcart full of cut sugar cane.

There by the cafe window, he parked and, as he was getting out of the car, a man with dirty clothes and broken, thick-framed glasses approached him.

"*Oye*, brother, *hace días que no como*," the man told Xavier, meaning that it'd been days since he'd eaten. "*¿No me puedes dar unos centavitos...para completar?*"

Xavier gave the man a dollar and walked away. As he passed another man at the entrance of the restaurant, a man selling flowers at the corner said to him, "Everybody thinks that guy's crazy, but he's making a killing asking people for money."

Xavier climbed the steps.

The man said behind him, "Shit, he's making more than me. Here I am busting my ass trying to sell my flowers."

Inside, the host greeted Xavier and sat him in the non-smoking section. The man left him a menu. A bus-boy brought over water and a basket of buttered bread.

The place was packed with people, mostly families and couples, getting through an early dinner.

The waitress, a woman as old as Xavier's mother, came over and asked him what he wanted. Xavier ordered a beer and the grilled red snapper with rice and fried plantains.

"Good choice," the waitress said. "The fish is very fresh today."

She was wearing a white *guayabera*, ink-stained at the pockets, and blue polyester pants. This was the wait-ing staff's uniform.

The waitress smiled at him and said, "Anything else? Dessert for afterwards? *¿Un cafecito?*"

"Thank you," he said.

She walked away.

The busboy brought Xavier the beer, poured it into an ice-cold glass, and quickly went to another table to pour water.

The movement fascinated Xavier as he drank his beer and looked on. The food didn't take long to arrive. The waitress set down the plates in front of him and said, "If you change your mind about the dessert, let me know." Again, she smiled at him and walked away.

Xavier ate with gusto, took his time eating as he watched the people come and go in the restaurant. After he finished the food, instead of ordering another beer, he ordered an espresso and drank it. After he paid the bill, he drove home, fed Brandy, and took her outside.

The sun set as Xavier sat in the yard. Brandy lay at his feet. The orange glow of the sky reflected off the dark canal water. A faint buzzing came from the banks. With a splash, a big fish broke the surface of the water.

Xavier stretched out his legs. He looked down at their shape.

Step in the right direction.

Hard to take.

Must go forward. Always.

Find a new identity.

Skin don't shed.

The years pass.

Those you can never regain.

Don't look back.

Change is hard.

You can no longer get by by merely adapting.

Break free. Search harder if you have to.

It can't be done, not here.

No, not here...

Vague was the history of his childhood. A man named Carlos Antonio Cuevas married a woman named Mirna Alarcón. They had been married for two years when Mirna got pregnant. Things were changing in their country. Political unrest. In 1962 they had their son and everything changed. They left the island and came to the United States.

This was the frame of his past. No stake in the old country, no deep roots to sever. He was an infant when they left. Though he spoke Spanish with his parents, English became his language of choice. His father spoke English well in the old country; his mother learned it here. They spoke it at home sometimes.

At school no one ever made fun of him because he didn't look like an outsider. An immigrant. A wetback. He fit in and so the children left him alone. That was the beginning of the transition in the unbalance of identity. More American, less Cuban. He was second generation. For all practical purposes, he got by, and that was the problem.

This was his place. His country. He'd been here ninety-nine percent of his life; but the one percent couldn't be ignored. Obviously, that one percent made all the difference.

It was now dark and the insects swarmed in full force. Xavier heard the mosquitos buzz around his head, looking for a place to land. They had already bitten him in a couple of places.

His blood was changing...

The phone rang inside. Xavier hurried to the kitchen because he wasn't sure how many times it had rung. Brandy followed him. He answered.

"Sorry, bro," Wilfredo said.

"No problem."

"Remember that marine biologist?"

Xavier listened.

"She was here and, man, did we have fun."

Brandy drank water and again lay at Xavier's feet.

Wilfredo continued, "She's too much. I don't know, I guess she gets lonely out at sea."

"At sea?"

Xavier looked at the fish bowl on the window sill. In it, as Xavier came closer, the fish floated on its side, at the bottom. It was dead.

"Shit," Xavier said, and held the bowl in his free hand and shook it.

"What?"

"Nothing," Xavier told him, then dumped the contents of the bowl into the sink.

"Anyway," Wilfredo said, "she does research out there."

"Ah," he said.

"Anyway, sorry. Have you eaten?"

"Sure did."

"I'm starving."

"Go out to eat."

"Join me for a couple of drinks?"

"Naw, I think I'll stay in and call it a night."

"That's a good plan," Wilfredo said, "Maybe I'll order in."

"I'll be in the office tomorrow."

"Meet you there."

"No," Xavier told him. "I have to see Eloísa in Kendall."

"Maybe we can have lunch."

"We can do that."

"See you tomorrow."

Everybody is where they should be, doing as always. Nothing changes unless you become the catalyst.

Xavier hung up. He went upstairs, turned on the TV, and removed his clothes. He climbed in bed and propped himself up on some pillows. After a while, Brandy ran up the stairs and jumped in bed with him. She curled up at his feet and fell asleep.

It'd been a long time since he'd stayed up late to watch television, but he couldn't sleep. Brandy snored at his feet. It was as close as he'd ever come to turning himself off. He guessed that's why so many people watched.

After Johnny Carson and David Letterman, after the news on CNN and Headline News, after the animal shows on the Discovery Channel, after all the stupid and nonsensical music videos on MTV and VH1, after the true-to-life crime and cop shows, after the black and white movie on the Classics Channel, after the reruns of shows he'd watched as a kid, after all that, America lost its soul.

Infomercials came on. People selling useless gadgets. There was the man with the food dehydrator which could also be used to make candied turkey gravy, the pasta machine that made pasta in all the colors of the rainbow, and the bagel slicer, and the tomato peeler, the old sports stars selling collapsible, easy to carry golf clubs and miracle pain medicines and ten easy steps to a powerful swing either on the golf course or on the tennis court, and fallen movie stars selling autographed posters and memorabilia, and singers plugging their perfume lines, and how their success was foretold by psychics on psychic lines, the diet/weight-loss/exercise methods, workshops, and equipment, and all the nine-seven-six numbers, heavily made-up women wanting to be your friend if only you'd call them for your private, personal message, and all the religious shows.

Ah, the religious shows, people being healed instantly by a mere touch and push of the head. Healed by prayer. Cured of all their sins by suave, smooth talkers with deep southern accents. But no one saved more souls than the man with the expensive suit whose expertise was to pray over a mound of letters. "Send more money," he said with his eyes closed, "send more money, send more money. I can feel the healing, but you must send more money!"

Xavier took a deep breath, gripped the remote control, and turned off the TV. Brandy stretched at his feet and then went back to sleep. It was dark in the room and still Xavier couldn't succumb to sleep. He tried. Tossed and turned. All along kept his eyes closed and listened to the quick rhythm of his heart on the pillow.

Enough to drive anyone crazy.

Early the next morning, Xavier woke up and felt as though he'd been beaten up. He didn't feel up to this new day, but he also knew that he couldn't stay in. He didn't want to stay alone in the house.

In the kitchen, he put coffee on to brew and fed Brandy, then went upstairs, showered, and dressed in work clothes. No tie, though, he didn't feel like putting on a tie. The long-sleeved shirt and slacks felt comfortable enough, *as comfortable as I can feel in business clothes*. The first thing he needed to do was go by Eloísa's and then on to the office.

After he drank a cup of fresh coffee, Xavier looked up Eloísa in the address book in his briefcase. He thought he knew how to get there, but it'd been a long time. He copied the Kendall address down on a piece of paper and folded it into his shirt pocket.

Xavier refilled his cup with coffee, got in the car, and drove out to the expressway. *This early and there's already heavy traffic.* The cars on the on-ramp were not being allowed to merge.

Sipping, he hit the breaks and spilled some coffee on his shirt. He put the mug down and reached over for a Kleenex in the glove compartment. The stain remained no matter how much he wiped.

The traffic picked up pace now, opened up, and everyone drove by the problem: a stalled vehicle in the left lane, with its emergency lights flashing, no driver anywhere to be found.

It took him twenty minutes to get from Bird Road to the Kendall exit on 88th, which was Kendall Drive. The apartments in this area were maintained fairly well, all having home-owners associations which paid for things like landscaping and general upkeep. Definitely worth it, compared to those apartments he'd seen in places like Hialeah and North Miami.

At 117th by the turnpike, he made a left and drove up three blocks. Eloísa and Izquierdo lived in the Conquistador Arms. He drove up to the guard, stopped, and gave him the apartment number.

The guard called Eloísa, waited a moment, then turned to Xavier and asked him his name.

Xavier told him; the guard said, "Javier."

The security guard put down the receiver and told Xavier to go ahead. The visitors' parking was to the left.

Xavier parked, walked through the humidity of the parking lot, went up the stairs to the apartment and knocked. Eloísa quickly came to the door and opened it.

"*Muchacho*," she said, and kissed Xavier. "How good to see you."

"Yes," he said, "it's good to see you, too." He gave her his condolences.

"Come in," she said. "Coffee's brewed. I know you drink the American stuff."

"Eloísa, thanks, but I'm in a bit of a hurry."

"This early?" she said.

Eloísa, in mourning clothes, led him into the living room. Family pictures hung on all the walls. He didn't remember the place looking like this, with so many pictures, then he realized what Eloísa had done. She'd built a shrine to her life with Izquierdo.

She went into the kitchen and he heard her pouring the coffee. "You take yours with sugar, right?" she asked.

"One teaspoon please."

"Cream?"

"None," he said, and looked at all the flowers under a large portrait of Izquierdo.

She stirred in the sugar, placed the coffee on a tray, and brought the tray out to the living room. A subdued light came into the room and made Xavier relax. He sat down by the coffee table where Eloísa set the tray.

"Do you believe in reincarnation?" Eloísa asked him.

"I'm afraid I don't," he said.

"I do," she said, and sat down. "I think Izquierdo is right here with us."

He leaned forward and sipped the coffee, which was hot against the palms of his hand. A subtle fragrance lingered about this room and he couldn't quite place its source. A mild jasmine. He figured it must be Eloísa's perfume.

"I wanted to ask you," she said, "what I need to do with our policy."

"Oh, sure," he said. "I will contact the company and have them send you a form. If you need help filling it out, I'll be more than happy to help you. After you finish the form, you have to submit it with a death certificate."

"How simple it all sounds," she said, and offered a weak smile.

"You have enough to worry about," he said.

She sat back and drank from her cup. "Things have changed so much," she said.

Xavier sighed, feeling tongue-tied. Uncertain.

"The world is…" She stared at him. "This life is so cruel, Xavier. People are greedy. Evil exists and will always exist, and neither you nor I will change it. *Can* change it." Her voice sounded hurt as if what she had just said was a motto for her.

"Being a family man," he said, "I think I know what you mean."

"Family men suffer most," said Eloísa. "They are the ones whose lives seem to always end too soon."

This was the kind of wisdom experience taught. It was very honest and direct, so direct that it didn't quite help Xavier feel at ease.

Xavier sat in front of Eloísa and listened to what a tough life she'd had with Izquierdo. "And this country didn't help," she said. "This country has been nothing but a curse to us Cubans. Sure, it helped some people, people young like you, but the old and the sick…"

She was fighting back the tears and Xavier thought he couldn't do it, sit there and watch this woman fall apart.

"I must go," he said.

"Forgive me," she said.

"For what?"

"For taking up your time," she said.

"Oh, please…it's just that I have another appointment," he lied.

"I understand."

He stood to go.

"Help me," she said, "with the box he wanted you to have. It's too heavy for me."

"Sure," he said, and followed her to the master bedroom.

The box, as she pointed out, was by the night stand. On the night stand by the reading lamp there was the

Bible bookmarked in the middle by some reading glasses.

"You know," she said, "this athritis..."

Xavier bent over and picked up the box. It was heavy, and as he carried it out of the bedroom he thought about its contents.

"Thank you for doing this," Eloísa told him.

At the door he reminded her to call him if she needed help with anything, then struggled with the box down the stairs.

She was looking down at him as he crossed the parking lot toward the car, opened a back door and plopped the box on the seat. Eloísa waved at him and he waved back.

Then he got in the car and drove out.

After he left the premises, he didn't get very far. His curiosity about what was inside the box overwhelmed him. He pulled over and stopped the car by the side of the road.

Xavier reached back and opened the lid. Inside were books. Thick books. He lifted one out and read the cover. It was a volume of *La Enciclopedia de Cuba*. Izquierdo had left him these books.

Then an idea struck him. He turned off the engine, got out of the car and got in the back seat. He searched through the box, reading the spines on each volume until he found the one with the index. He turned to the end and searched for M. Under M, to his amazement and surprise, he spotted "Manteca, Sonny, Vol. 5, pg. 340."

He dug out Volume 5 (*Artes, Sociedad, Filosofía*) and turned to page 340. There on the page, next to pictures of Bola de Nieve, Beny Moré, and Dámaso Pérez Prado, was Sonny Manteca.

Xavier leaned back, turned the book to the light, and read:

SONNY MANTECA. (1926–1962). Musician. Perhaps known as the best *conga* player in the world, he was born and raised in the poorest section of Havana. He learned to play during the Great Depression. He played the instrument in his own tropical style, with gusto and zest. Rhythm was Manteca; Manteca was soul, *alma*, bravura, salsa, the mambo, the cha-cha-cha. Sonny—the magical mulatto, the epitome of his musical times, the king of the latin beat, the life-lover—Manteca. The greatest percussionist. Sonny died outside of Cuba, kept out by politics, a bitter and depressed exile. The day Sonny died, the music world lost its most vibrant, colorful and wonderful musician.

Xavier reread the entry...*died outside of Cuba, kept out by politics, a bitter and depressed exile.*

He looked at the black and white picture of the musician. It looked like a frame taken from a film clip. There on the scratched surface, the picture showed Sonny sitting on a stage with his *congas* between his legs, slapping away at their skins. Sonny sat there with his eyes closed as if in a trance, rhythm running through him like an electrical current.

The caption under the picture read, "*Mi dolor y mi placer*, what Sonny Manteca called his *congas*."

147

Xavier looked at the musician's hands. They were out of focus because of the captured movement. Blurred, they looked like two birds doing a mating dance on the surface of the skins.

This is the caress, the feel, the spiritual connection with the musical muses. Music, the only thing that keeps us alive and going...

Xavier decided to take the turnpike back to the office. That'd be the shortest route, and he was accustomed to short cuts. The turnpike's on-ramp forked, northbound on the left, southbound on the right. As Xavier signaled to go north, a car cut in front of him and in the heavy traffic didn't allow him to get in. Xavier was stuck—he stayed on the right and went south. He drove on looking for an exit to take and turn around, but something compelled him to keep going south.

He was driven by some kind of notion that if he kept going south, he'd come to something. He'd never been this far south and the landscape was quickly changing. He passed Cutler Ridge, Perrine, Homestead...in Homestead he reached down for his phone, but it wasn't there. Then he remembered seeing it back in the office.

He drove past Homestead and where the turnpike stopped and joined highway US 1. He kept going south. In Key Largo, he thought he needed to stop and call the office. He found a shopping center on the way and stopped. No phones anywhere. Then he saw the sign: **LAS CASUELAS DE MANUELA, Cuban Café & Seafood Restaurant**. Outside the place was a dog tied to a shopping cart full of bundles. He walked in. The place looked neither like a café nor a restaurant. It was a bar, long and deep.

Xavier entered it's penumbra.

The place was empty except for the woman behind the bar. She was watching a portable TV. From the sounds of the melodramatic Spanish, Xavier surmised a *novela*, the Spanish soap opera. The woman looked at him.

Way in the back of the place, by the paneled wall, stood a life-size statue of San Lázaro. He looked so real with his crutches, bleeding leprous sores. There was a life-size dog at his side, licking at his festering sores.

"Do you have a phone?" Xavier asked.

"In the back," she said, "by the bathrooms."

Xavier traveled the length of the bar and went past San Lázaro—someone had placed a plate of dark pennies and fruit at his feet—through a set of swinging doors, found the phone, put a coin in, and dialed the office. The operator came on to tell him that since this was a long distance call he'd have to put in more money. He dropped in all the change he had left.

The phone rang and the ringing sounded far away.

Darleen answered. "Cuevas Insurance," she said.

"Darleen, it's me, Xavier."

"Hi," she said.

"Any calls?"

"Nope."

"Any messages?"

"Nope."

"Is Wilfredo there?"

"Not here yet," she said.

Business as usual.

"What do you want me to do?" she asked. "I can tell him to call you."

He told her about his phone.

"Let me check," she said, and put him on hold.

Then his time was up and the phone clicked off. He returned to the bar and asked the woman, who was intently watching the screen, for change.

"For change," she said, "you've got to order something."

"Coffee," he said.

"Not done yet," she said.

"A beer."

"What kind."

"I don't care," he said.

She walked to the other end of the bar, opened the lid to the freezer, and brought him a beer. She uncapped it for him and then said, "Two-fifty."

Xavier gave her a five. "Please break the ones," he said.

"I don't have that much change," she said.

"I'll take whatever you have," he said.

"I can't do that. I'll be left with nothing."

Forget it, he thought, *I don't want to call back. What for?*

She put his change in front of him. He sipped the beer and sat down for a minute. Just to think about what to do next.

The woman returned to her television.

"Don't get much business out here," he said.

She didn't pay attention to him.

No wonder, he thought, and drank.

Next to him sat an old man. Xavier didn't know from where the old man had come, but suspected the man had been in the bathroom all along. Xavier eyed the man who was dressed in what looked like tattered, oil-stained clothes. His frail arms were full of bruises, or were they grease smudges?

"*Aquí no le dan ni migajas a uno*," the man said in Spanish, meaning that this place didn't even give away crumbs.

The woman looked over and gave Xavier a serious look. Xavier didn't know why he was staying, other than out of principle. He paid for his beer and he intended to finish it.

"Where you from?" the man asked.

"Miami," said Xavier.

"No, what country?"

"Here."

"No, you're not from here."

"My parents are Cuban," Xavier said.

"I'm Cuban," the old man said. "That's *all* I am."

"Down a long ways."

"Or up," he said. "Depends how you look at it."

Xavier glanced at the woman, but she was lost in the action on the screen. From where Xavier sat, the screen looked fuzzy, riddled with static.

"Do you know who I am?" the old man asked.

"I have no idea," Xavier said.

"Lázaro, *mi hermano.*"

Xavier turned and gazed at the old man. His hair was white, cropped short.

"And I am Cuban. Nothing but Cuban."

Crazy bastard, Xavier mused, *been out in the sun and heat too long. Panhandler. How will I shake this guy?*

"Actually," he said, "I don't exist."

"But you said you were Cuban."

"I am a Parable," he said.

"Right."

"I'm lost here, though."

"I'll give you money," Xavier said, and smiled, "to get you where you want to go."

"Very kind of you," the old man said.

Xavier finished the last of his beer and left the man the change on the bar. He got up and walked toward the front. The woman ignored him. At the entrance, Xavier opened the door and walked out into the sunshine. The dog and shopping cart were gone. Then he turned and looked back in. The bar was empty except for the woman and the life-size San Lázaro keeping the vigil in the back.

I don't know what to believe.

Once in the car, Xavier took off southbound.

Without a map or a compass, Xavier headed south to the southernmost point of the United States, born out of sand and water and palm trees and mangroves. The mangroves merged in a flickering blur of green as he sped. He drove with a great sense of urgency. The easterly salty winds blew inland from an opaque sea and swept and rocked the car as if it had, like a Spanish galleon, great billowing sails. He drove on.

Behind him lay a city of spirits long turned to rubble, dust, grass, and soft earth. He sped down this river of ruin and tar and encrusted possum and armadillo carcasses, and rain. A car became a beige speck on the horizon where the blue of the sky met the ground in the shimmering distance, caught in splendor among the tall weeds and grass.

Motor oil veined the divided asphalt. Cars and trucks hummed and buzzed past. *So many lives destroyed and more on the brink. This is the end of the road that connects North and South with a single thread of loneliness and disillusionment.*

This road leads to the southernmost point…

No time left to forget from where the wind blew him like a tumbleweed.

It was hot, even in the air-conditioned car which seemed to be running out of freon. On the way, Xavier kept track of the names of the keys: Tavernier, Isla Morada, Upper and Lower Matacumbe, Long Key, Duck Key, Marathon, Bahia Honda, Big Pine, Ramrod Key... what alluring sounds.

The day was bright and sunny. Not a cloud on the magnificent sky. Xavier had never seen with such clarity. "Welcome to the Florida Keys," the signs read.

DON'T SPEED: It is better to arrive late than not to arrive at all!

In the Keys, life lingered like a slug, beat to a slow beat across nowhere but marshlands and a seven-mile bridge that reached further than the eye could see, past liquor stores, banks, fast-food restaurants, gift shops, tourist traps, sea-shell motels and dead-hour resorts.

Within city limits now, Xavier yearned for a way to be somewhere else.

He drove on.

This was the southernmost point of the mainland United States, and the hum inside the car whispered.

He arrived and parked by the side of the road. He got out of the car and walked over to the spot with the red- and white-painted bouy. The sign told him he had arrived, indeed. This was the end of the road.

The island of his birth lay 90 miles away. Xavier remembered some of his clients saying that they drove down here because on clear, windless nights, one could see the lights from Havana.

At the edge, where the asphalt ran out and turned into rocks and sand and the water started, Xavier stood and gazed at the open sea.

In the water, he swam, taking wide, long strokes. He moved away from the land, leaving all his troubles behind...

A voice speaking in a foreign tongue startled him. Xavier turned to the voice. It was a man with a camera. The man, fat and dressed in shorts and a T-shirt, nose anointed with sunscreen, sunglasses on, a hat, was telling him something in what sounded like German.

The man *was* a German tourist, down here with his family, trying to take a group portrait, but he couldn't because Xavier was in the way of the background view.

"Bitte, gehen Sie aus dem Weg!" the man said.

In the awkward foreignness of the situation, Xavier couldn't understand.

"Vielen dank."

Then, Xavier Cuevas turned to the sea and, clothes and all, dove off and plunged into the water. He went under, opened his eyes to the sting of the salt, held his breath, and swam.

In the pursuit of the unattainable, Xavier Cuevas was swimming home.